LADY JANE HAD EVERYTHING SHE COULD WANT. ALMOST.

Lady Jane had the memory of Richard—tender, sensitive, caring—whose life she had intended to share before that life was tragically ended.

Lady Jane had the fortune Richard had left her, a fortune that made her independent of the necessity of seeking any man to provide for her.

Lady Jane had the example of her younger sister, Nancy, who had made what seemed a perfect marriage only to find herself in fearful bondage.

In short, Lady Jane had everything she could want to enjoy single bliss.

Until she met the haughty, self-centered, and unfortunately all-too-attractive Viscount Rossmere and began to sense what she was missing—no matter how dangerous it might be to have. . . .

DUELS OF THE HEART

THE
PROUD
VISCOUNT

by

Laura Matthews

A SIGNET BOOK

NEW AMERICAN LIBRARY

For Paul, Laura, and Matt,
who knew I could do it

NAL BOOKS ARE AVAILABLE AT QUANTITY DISCOUNTS
WHEN USED TO PROMOTE PRODUCTS OR SERVICES.
FOR INFORMATION PLEASE WRITE TO PREMIUM MARKETING DIVISION.
NEW AMERICAN LIBRARY. 1633 BROADWAY.
NEW YORK. NEW YORK 10019.

Copyright © 1987 by Elizabeth Rotter

SIGNET TRADEMARK REG. U.S. PAT. OFF. AND FOREIGN COUNTRIES
REGISTERED TRADEMARK—MARCA REGISTRADA
HECHO EN CHICAGO. U.S.A.

SIGNET, SIGNET CLASSIC, MENTOR, ONYX, PLUME,
MERIDIAN and NAL BOOKS are published by NAL PENGUIN INC.,
1633 Broadway, New York, New York 10019

First Printing, May, 1987

1 2 3 4 5 6 7 8 9

PRINTED IN THE UNITED STATES OF AMERICA

1

"He'll have to marry money, of course."

Mabel Reedness announced this truth as though it were something that might have escaped her niece's notice. For most of her forty-five years, Mabel had prided herself on being forthright. More recently she believed herself to have developed considerable matchmaking skills, which mainly meant that she was fond of reminding everyone that it had been she who introduced Jane's sister Nancy to her husband.

"Not that he should have the least trouble finding a wife, mind you. He's truly a fine figure of a man, and his title, though only a viscountcy, is nothing to scoff at."

Lady Jane, in her usual calm manner, agreed that it was so. She could see his lordship through the open doors of the summer parlor, galloping toward the Home Wood on Ascot. She rather wished Lord Rossmere hadn't brought Ascot with him. A year's time had not managed to heal that particular wound.

"Having to marry where there's a fortune is a distressing thing for a man of his pride," Mabel continued. "Still, for five-and-thirty he's quite a well-favored fellow. I'm surprised he doesn't have half a dozen young ladies dangling after him."

"That would be difficult," Lady Jane remarked dryly. "He doesn't take the least interest in London society."

"But he can't afford to!" Mabel picked up the fringe she'd been knotting and regarded it with disfavor. "He won't even accept all the help I've offered. Frankly, I consider that a trifle *too* proud in a godchild. There would be nothing wrong in my lending him a little blunt to put on a show in London for a Season, but he'll accept nothing more than necessary money for the Longborough Park mortgage."

Rossmere had cleared the hedgerow that separated Willow End's lawns from the Home Wood. Jane watched as he directed Ascot along the path that skirted the wood, riding the magnificent beast with incredible ease. After the accident, Jane had considered having the horse destroyed, but Richard's will had specifically instructed that Rossmere was to have Ascot. When the horse's various injuries healed, it was a relief to send him away from Willow End.

Horse and rider disappeared from sight and Lady Jane tried to concentrate on what her aunt was saying. Mabel's voice had taken on a note of urgency. "The thing is, he won't look for a wife. I've tried to talk with him about it, but he refuses to hear a word on the subject. And if he doesn't marry, the title will die with him. He's the last of the line."

"Perhaps if Lord Rossmere had something for a future generation to inherit, he'd be more inclined to produce an heir. As it is . . ." Jane shrugged her shoulders. "Why bother?"

Mabel dismissed this eminently practical view of the situation, knowing that her niece, daughter of an earl, could not possibly believe it for a moment. Jane's opinions were a bit odd at times, but not that odd. She couldn't always tell when Jane was teasing her, because her niece's hazel eyes were always as clear and guileless as those of a child, and her ready smile held no hint of duplicity.

"He still has the estate, sadly deteriorated and encumbered though it may be. Longborough Park was a splendid pile twenty years ago. I wish you could have seen it then. But his father with the gambling fever . . . Well, least said, of course. When I think of all the rooms shut up, the furniture in holland covers, the stables empty, the staff down to a few old retainers . . ."

"Exactly," said Jane bracingly. "It would be better for the title and land to revert to the crown, so it might be given to someone with wealth who could restore it. That's the problem with all this entailment business, Aunt Mabel. Any ordinary person would be able to sell the crumbling ruins and buy himself a little cottage in the Lake District with the profits."

Now Mabel was sure her niece was jesting; Jane had no more use for cottages than for crumbling piles. But only a hint of sparkle in the hazel eyes gave the younger woman away. "You're trying to distract me," she scolded, giving the younger woman a scowl. "This is a very serious matter, my dear girl, and I won't be sidetracked by your absurd suggestions. I have arrived at a solution to the problem for him."

"It's usually best to let people solve their own problems."

"I've never found it to be true. Left to his own devices, Rossmere wouldn't do a thing about finding himself a wife." She picked at the fringe in her lap, not meeting Jane's eyes. "Nor would you do a thing about finding yourself a husband."

Jane shook her head with fond exasperation. "You know I have no intention of marrying, dear Aunt Mabel. And I'm sure Lord Rossmere isn't interested in allying himself with a twenty-eight-year-old spinster who's very nearly as tall as he is and who hasn't a classical feature to her name. I beg you to drop this scheme before you make some mischief."

"Mischief!" Mabel snorted. "What could be more eligible than a marriage between my niece and my godson? Both from the most distinguished families; both very attractive people. So what if you are tall? You have an elegance a shorter woman wouldn't dare lay claim to. And as for your age, so much the better. I'm sure Rossmere has no use for schoolroom chits."

"How could you possibly know that?"

"He's an intelligent man. I have no patience with this theory that an unformed, mewling girl can best be shaped to a man's taste. More likely she'll remain an unformed, mewling girl who hasn't the first idea how to run a home or deal with a husband's idiosyncrasies." Mabel met her niece's amused eyes. "Besides, young girls are romantics. That could be a great nuisance. They wouldn't necessarily understand the finer points of marrying an impoverished viscount, or undertaking the restoration of a fine old mansion."

Jane didn't try to restrain a chuckle. "I doubt if anyone understands the finer points of marrying an impoverished viscount. But that's not the half of it. It's an altogether unworkable plan, my dear, and you must abandon it before you embarrass me, to say nothing of Lord Rossmere."

Mabel's jaw developed a stubborn set. "You must marry and have children. It's the most important thing in a woman's life."

"Oh, pooh. I'm an aunt ten times over already, and godmother twice. That's more than enough children on whom to lavish my affections."

"It's not the same. Believe me, I know."

It was a bit of a shock for Jane to hear Mabel confess that being an aunt wasn't enough. Within the family it had always been assumed that she was content to be the spinster aunt of her brother's five motherless children.

She had, after all, lived with them most of her adult life, since Jane's mother died after Nancy's birth.

For a moment Jane couldn't think how best to reply. The sluggish murmur of the hot August afternoon whispered through the open doors. Finally Jane moved to tug at the bell cord. "I'll have Winters bring us some cold lemonade."

"Yes, that would be nice." Mabel cleared her throat. "And then there's the matter of your inheritance."

"I beg your pardon?" Jane had inherited Richard's estate, Graywood, along with all his other worldly possessions, except Ascot.

"There are those who think it wrong for you to have inherited Richard's estate when you were never married to him."

Jane's brows rose. "Surely you aren't influenced by that kind of talk. Richard had every right to leave me his property, if he chose to."

Mabel stared straight out the open doorway. "Yes, but property is always transferred through a will, and a will states that its author is of sound mind."

"Richard was quite sane when he drew up the will."

"I know that and you know that, but there are those who doubt it. If a man has spells of insanity, can he ever be adjudged completely sane?"

An angry retort rose to Jane's lips, but it was forestalled by the entrance of the butler. She gave instructions for lemonade and queen cakes and watched Winters depart in silence.

Mabel had taken up the fringe again and concentrated her attention on it as she spoke. "You've always been a woman of property, Jane, through your mother, and there will be considerably more one day when your father passes on. You really have no need of Richard's property."

"In our imperfect world, inheritance is not based on need."

"True. And I quite understand why Richard left you his property. He loved you and would have married you had it been possible. For that love and the suffering it caused you, you deserve every mite of his property."

"But . . . ?"

"But if Richard had left no will, his property would have gone to Rossmere as his nearest relation. In fact, the will stated that if you died before Richard, his property was to go to Rossmere." Mabel sighed, a gusty, soulful exhalation. "I'm not saying Rossmere believes he should have come into the property, Jane. I'm saying that it would have been better if he had. And there's still a way he can."

"Nonsense. If Richard had wanted Rossmere to have his property, he had only to will it to him. I never asked Richard to make me his beneficiary. It was something he wanted to do. He wasn't responsible for Rossmere's predicament. In fact, Rossmere wasn't even the viscount when Richard originally made the will. Or the codicil giving him Ascot. Richard simply never changed it after Rossmere's troubles began."

"Did you ever suggest that he should?"

"It never occurred to me." Jane rose abruptly and wandered restlessly around the room. "I hardly know Rossmere, Aunt Mabel. At most I've seen him half a dozen times since I became an adult. I had enough things on my mind without worrying about his financial straits. If I thought of him at all while Richard was alive, I suppose I thought he would marry an heiress. After all, he has the title."

"If you had told Richard you didn't want his property, that he should leave it to Rossmere, he would have done it."

"I didn't know Richard was going to die so young!" Jane cried. "I thought there was all the time in the world. I thought we would continue loving each other until we grew old, and that I could even marry him when my childbearing years were past. In the dark times, when he was under restraint, I tried to think of him as little as possible. His will meant nothing more to me than a pledge of his devotion."

Jane could still vividly recall the only discussion they'd ever had of his making a will. Richard had just recovered from the first episode of his madness, and his face remained pale, his eyes haunted. They sat on the bank of the stream that ran through his property, her hand held tightly between both of his.

"You understand this means we can't marry, don't you?" he'd asked. She had thought her heart would break. "My father became progressively more . . . disturbed. That could happen to me, too, Jane, so I'm making my will now, while I'm perfectly capable of it. You're to have everything, just as though we'd married. It will be a symbol of my love for you, something tangible for the world to see."

She had been too upset to discuss the matter. And his condition had not deteriorated, as they had feared. In between episodes of madness he had been as lucid as ever, and she had thought he would live to be an old, old man. Perhaps he would have, if not for the fall from Ascot. Or had the fall itself been caused by an approaching episode? Had one of his pounding headaches come over him while he was riding? Had it come too quickly, engulfing him with self-destructive violence before he could reach safety? Oh, why hadn't she been there?

The sound of hoofbeats filtered into the room again and the two women turned to watch Rossmere canter alongside the Home Wood back toward the stable. Richard had once told Jane that the viscount had the best seat he'd ever seen, and he was certainly an impressive figure on horseback. Beast and man seemed to move as one, with the wind streaming through Ascot's mane and Rossmere's wavy black hair. Their bodies flowed in perfect rhythm, Rossmere's hands steady on the reins, his thighs tightly gripped against the animal.

For one stunning moment Jane felt furious with him. Who was Rossmere to ride Ascot with such careless ease when Richard had met his death on the huge brute? Why should the viscount bemoan his lack of fortune when he was alive and sane and titled? He could easily marry a fortune if he would tame his pride a little. Richard would remain dead in the Graywood graveyard, no matter what.

Jane turned her head from the sight of Rossmere on Ascot and willed away the irrational resentment. It wasn't Rossmere's fault that Richard was dead. Still, there was something about the viscount that distressed her, and had from the moment he'd walked in the front door of Willow End two days ago.

It might have been his pride. He radiated a self-containment that kept everyone else at a distance. It wasn't that he was lacking in manners; far from it. He was punctiliously polite, but lacking the warmth and closeness common in Jane's family. His holding himself apart contributed to the impression that he was proud, perhaps even arrogant. Jane might have conceded that this was a disguise adopted because of his penury. Except for his eyes.

Rossmere's eyes were a remarkable shade of silver blue. Though the color was distinctive, it was not the most significant thing about his eyes. They were bone-chillingly cold, like the silver-blue sky of a freezing winter's day. And there was a power in them, an authority, that disturbed Jane even more.

She turned to her aunt now and laid a hand on her arm. "I'll give some thought to the inheritance and whether I might in some manner share it with Lord Rossmere. I really have no need of it for myself. But you mustn't pursue this idea of an alliance. His lordship is not someone with whom I'd be interested in forming a connection, even if I were considering marriage."

Winters entered with the lemonade and queen cakes and set them on a gateleg table near where the ladies were seated. Jane thanked and dismissed him before speaking again. "I know it's been a year since Richard died, but I'm not ready to think of marrying. I may never be."

"But you must! You'll regret it all your life if you don't."

"Perhaps." She offered the plate of queen cakes to her aunt. "I'd rather not discuss it any further, Aunt Mabel. Would you help me plan the menu for Saturday's dinner party?"

The older woman eyed her with frustration, but lifted her thin shoulders. "I don't consider the matter settled," she informed her niece, "but I'm willing to let it rest for the time being."

Jane escaped to the circular conservatory, where no one would think to look for her. A winged statue of a nude woman, the replica of one of her father's favorite antiquarian finds, stood in a niche opposite huge pots holding profusely blooming plants. The moist, stifling air in the room was almost unbearable. Jane pushed damp tendrils of brown hair from her forehead, thinking it would have been wiser to disappear to the dairy on a day like this.

She seated herself on a bench in the only shaded window. Larkspur and verbena thrust bright flowers out of containers on either side of her, and vines wound from floor to ceiling all around the room. At this time of year the conservatory looked like a gigantic garden basket, filled with the brightest and sweetest-smelling flowers that grew at Willow End. The horse chestnut outside the window filtered a green light into the room and tinted her white jaconet muslin dress.

The letter from Trelenny Ashwicke was still in her pocket. She'd been about to read it when Mabel interrupted her. Now she drew it out and spread it on her lap. As she read, a smile played around her lips and lit her eyes. Dear Trelenny! Nothing was ever going to tame her high spirits, thank heaven. Fortunately Cranford had realized in time that he loved her for them, rather than in spite of them. It seemed forever since she'd been with them in Bath, and yet it was little more than a year ago. Jane had intended to make the journey for their wedding, and would have, if Richard hadn't died.

Richard. How easy it was for everyone else to forget him. Jane had even heard her aunt and her father using terms like "for the best" when they didn't know she overheard them. Nothing would ever convince her that his death was for the best.

But Mabel might be right about Richard's estate. Rossmere certainly would have benefited from inheriting it. What would he have done with it, though? Its only use to him would be in the money a sale would bring. Jane couldn't bear the thought of strangers owning Graywood. Even now it was hard for her to see the tenants there when she rode past. When their lease was up next month, she would have to decide if she should renew it for another year. Or could she possibly . . . ? No, it would cause far too much gossip for her to try to move there alone. She turned her gaze toward the window.

Rossmere had stopped under the horse chestnut on his way from the stables to the house. He stood unmoving, except for toying with a furry horse chestnut in one hand. He was not looking in her direction, and she had no way of knowing whether he'd seen her. Somehow she doubted it. His face wore a thoughtful look, with the eyes narrowed slightly and the lips pursed. It was a handsome face, as her aunt had said. He was a much larger man than Richard—not just taller, but more muscular and substantial. Even his hands looked stronger, as though they could crush the hard chestnut to pulp.

Perhaps it was the coiled strength in him that disturbed

Jane. She expected it in a horse, energy ready to be released at the urging of hands or heels. In a man it seemed much more dangerous, an unknown quantity. Did it indicate a terrible temper, or an abundance of energy, or a touch of madness? Jane shook off such fanciful thoughts. Obviously they were only ramblings of her mind, evoked by her reminiscences of Richard. Rossmere was solid and healthy and undoubtedly as sane as the next man.

With surprising speed, he swung back his arm and threw the chestnut at a gate some distance away. His aim was accurate. The horse chestnut smacked into the upper rail and dropped to the ground. Rossmere continued to frown after it for some time before strolling off toward the hall.

Jane forced her gaze back to Trelenny's letter. Perhaps she would go to visit the Ashwickes as her friend suggested . . . after Lord Rossmere left Willow End, taking Ascot with him.

2

Lord Rossmere returned to the house with some reluctance. His godmother, Lady Mabel Reedness, had specifically requested his presence in the north drawing room at four o'clock, and Rossmere barely had time to make himself presentable. Without Lady Mabel he would have been ruined years ago. She had lent him money when every banker he approached had refused him a loan. Rossmere suffered considerably under his burden of gratitude to Lady Mabel.

For some time he had managed to find excuses for turning down her invitations to visit Willow End, but he was in a financial bind again. There was another mortgage payment coming due, and improvements that simply had to be carried out on the estate if he was ever to lift himself out of debt. It would have been grossly uncivil of him to expect his godmother to provide the money he needed while at the same time refusing to accept her hospitality for a month.

For some reason it hadn't even occurred to him that bringing Ascot would upset everyone, from Lord Barlow down to the stable hands. "Not to be trusted," was the way they were given to phrasing it. What they meant was that Richard had met his death riding that horse, and no one was sure whether the horse or Richard's illness was to blame. They preferred to think it was the horse. Rossmere had ridden Ascot for the last year, and he knew better.

The horse was half-wild, of course. Always had been. Rossmere remembered riding him several years ago when he'd visited Richard. There was no sign during his "good" times that Richard was sick at all. Actually, Rossmere had considered Ascot the sole indication. An odd concept, perhaps, but one he felt quite certain about. Ascot was infected with the untamed wildness that seized Richard during the black times. In the man this primitive turbulence was horrifying; in the horse it was awesome.

Ascot's wildness was not a challenge to him. Rossmere had no interest in "conquering" the beast, or mastering its unruly temper. Quite the opposite, in fact. His blood raced with the excitement of allowing Ascot his head, of storming across fields and soaring over fences at a speed and height he'd not known before, even in his younger years, when the best of horses were available to him.

Rossmere liked to remember Richard in the "good" times, riding Ascot as he himself did now, filled with the glory of unrestricted movement. But he never forgot that Richard didn't always have that freedom. From the first sign of an impending episode, he was locked safely in the farthest wing of Willow End, cared for by a stout manservant and no other. If Rossmere had wondered why Richard was imprisoned at Willow End and not his own estate of Graywood, he had never given voice to his question.

For this visit Rossmere had been given a suite in the east wing. Both the sitting room and the bedroom were hung with tapestries depicting various Greek and Roman myths, their predominant colors of brown and blue heavy against the tan walls. Various details lightened the rooms, though: the vases of summer flowers, the light draperies at the windows, the height and intricacy of the ceilings.

While he allowed Lord Barlow's valet to adjust the fit of his coat, he gazed out over the park where the ground rose toward the downs. They had raced there once, he and Richard. Ascot had triumphed over his own hack without the slightest difficulty, and Rossmere had found himself longing to ride the huge black stallion. As though aware of his thoughts, a tendency Richard exhibited from time to time, he'd dismounted and beckoned the viscount to take over Ascot. "You'll do well with him," he'd said, though the general wisdom at the Graywood and Willow End stables even in those days was that no one but Richard could manage the wild horse. No doubt it was that incident that had prompted Richard to add the codicil to his will giving Rossmere the horse.

Because everything else had gone to Lady Jane.

For one brief moment, when the letter came from his godmother informing him of Richard's death, he had allowed himself to hope that he would be his cousin's beneficiary, that all his financial embarrassments were over. That tiny, suspended moment between reading one sentence and the next had betrayed him. To have considered his own situation when his poor cousin lay dead might have been human, but it disgusted him, showing him how poverty had eroded his humanity. Rossmere had vowed then that it wouldn't happen again.

As he strode through the corridors of the house, he caught glimpses of the small army of servants who kept the place immaculate. He'd been raised to that kind of luxury, where his every whim was accommodated and his pockets were perpetually full. He was reduced now to two loyal family retainers who served him at Longborough Park, but he'd found that there were certain compensations for his present position.

One of them was that he wasn't expected to fulfill any social obligations.

There were no balls, and few parties, that he regretted not attending, and he certainly didn't mind not having to give them himself. He regretted not being able to maintain a stable of riding and carriage horses, and he wished there were the resources to hunt, but he preferred the freedom of his run-down seat to the straitlaced strictures of London . . . or even of Willow End.

He presented himself now to Lady Mabel with his usual polite attention. She was seated on a spoon-back chair that looked only marginally comfortable, though there were plenty of more commodious seats in the room. Her graying hair was pulled back tightly into a bun and her posture was rigid with resolution. She waved him imperatively to a chair and regarded him with a penetrating stare. Calculated to remind him of his indebtedness? Perhaps. He had only known her to be forthright, not manipulative. It was possible that she merely assessed him.

"I saw you on Ascot," she said. "There's a devil in the beast that's not always controllable."

"So I've noticed. I assure you I don't underestimate him."

"Good." She dismissed the subject with a slight flip of her hand. "I wanted you to come here so we could have a talk about your future, Rossmere."

Though he disliked the sound of this topic, he continued to look agreeable, without offering a remark or asking a question. He was not a man to be easily intimidated. His godmother was forced to continue her discussion without his help.

"There's the matter of my family obligations. I have five nieces and nephews in addition to you, my godchild. When I die, my brother's children have some right to expect an inheritance from me. Not that they need it, any of them, but they're blood ties. I'd feel more comfortable knowing that each of them was already provided for, and there's one who isn't, in some ways. Jane may have more than sufficient property, but she lacks that essential for any woman—a husband and family."

"It's most unfortunate Lady Jane was unable to marry Richard." Rossmere knew precisely where his aunt was headed now and he refused to follow her there. He had been away from society too long. It hadn't occurred to him, when the invitation came from Lady Mabel, that she would have this particular scheme in mind, though it should have. She had been determined for years to marry him off to an heiress. He was surprised she would consider her own niece, except for Lady Jane's advanced age. Rossmere regarded his godmother with a slight frown of disapproval. "I don't think she has recovered from my cousin's death."

"She may never," Mabel informed him in her bluntest manner. "That's hardly the point. Each month that passes reduces her chance of marrying. We're not talking about a love match. We're speaking strictly of a marriage of convenience. For both of you, Rossmere. You need a wife who has property. Jane needs a husband who can establish a place for her in society and give her children."

"I can't believe your niece would countenance such a match."

"Perhaps not—just yet." Mabel leaned toward him, gripping the arms of her chair with determined fingers. "You would have to convince her of the desirability of the match. She thinks she will be content as an aunt to her brothers' and sisters' children. It's not enough. She needs to marry soon, before she can become entrenched in a spinster's way of life."

"What else has she been leading all these years?"

Mabel bestowed a scornful look on him. "Basically she's led the life of a fiancée these past seven years. A fiancée who never intended to marry, it's true, but a fiancée nonetheless. With all that entails."

Rossmere couldn't be sure exactly what his godmother meant to convey by this insistence on a pseudo-engagement. Surely not that the young woman wasn't a virgin. After all, the reason the pair hadn't wed was because of the possibility of her becoming pregnant with yet another mentally disturbed Bower. Richard Bower's father had suffered from the illness; his son would likely have inherited the same weakness.

No, Lady Jane was undoubtedly as pure as any other young lady of refinement. Her aunt was merely indicating that there had been no possibility of her considering another man as a husband because of her intense attachment to Richard. Well, Rossmere could credit that, but it carried no weight with him in this argument.

"Your niece is a very fine young woman," he told Mabel. "But I have no intention of marrying and I'm sure she wouldn't have a pauper for a husband in any case. No woman of sensibility would. So let's make an end to this project of yours, ma'am. Lady Jane wouldn't thank you for it."

"I'm convinced she would eventually." Mabel sighed her impatience and plucked at the skirts of her gray Circassian cloth dress. "She needs something, someone, to make her forget Richard. She's withdrawn from us this past year. An outsider might be a good distraction. Please, at least spend some time with her."

"Of course." Rossmere rose and laid a hand on Mabel's shoulder. "I can't be a suitor, but I can offer diversion. I was very fond of Richard, and your niece made his life worth living those last years. For his sake as well as yours, I'll be happy to help."

Mabel nodded, and thanked him. Rossmere hurriedly excused himself before a new line of attack should occur to his godmother. This was not the time to put forth his request for another loan. He bowed gracefully and strolled toward the door. He'd almost made it when she called out, "Your mother would have hated to see the title die out, Rossmere. And your father even more so. It's a responsibility beyond the individual, a duty to your heritage and your country. It's your own pride that's standing in the way, my dear boy, and that's no credit to you in this instance."

Rossmere paused and directed a quelling stare at his godmother. "I think I have to be the one to decide on such personal matters, ma'am. If my decision doesn't agree with the general opinion of the *ton*, I won't be the least alarmed. It's a great pity the title will become extinct with me, but then it's a great pity there aren't the funds to carry off the position with authority. If you will excuse me."

He set a quick pace down the corridor to the doorway leading to the east garden. This area was sheltered from view by hedges on two sides, probably to provide a windless area in which to walk on blustery days. Willow End was rich in such amenities, as Longborough Park had been. There wasn't even a decent walk on his estate now. Plantings of a decorative nature had become overgrown, since they called for more expenditure than he could afford. Well, what was the use of comparisons? These days there was no comparison between the ravaged Longborough Park and the beautiful Willow End.

The gravel crunched under his feet as he paced down the walk. He scarcely noticed the abundance of blooms that lined his path. His mind was on other matters, particularly this scheme of his aunt's with regard to Lady Jane. She was not at all his style of woman. Rossmere had never come close to marrying, even before his father managed to gamble away practically every penny of what should have been his patrimony. Rossmere found the women of his social class profoundly boring.

The type of woman he was attracted to was not some tame thing, trained to play the pianoforte and manage a household competently. She was a flamboyant woman, beautiful and amusing. Outrageous in her outlook on life. Someone who could laugh at the rules, who had the intelligence to see beyond the little parlor games society played. Someone who felt a real excitement about living each day. Rossmere had never met a woman of his class who matched this description.

But he had once had a mistress who did.

That was in the old days, though. It had been a long time since he'd been able to afford the luxury of a mistress. Not that any physical need would drive him to take a wife now. He had no wish to put himself under an obligation to any woman, except the necessary one to his godmother. If he married a rich woman, the weight of his indebtedness would crush him. It didn't matter that he would be offering a title in exchange, or that legally the property would become his. Rossmere had a very deep sense of pride, and it didn't allow him the latitude of a less-principled man. The possibility that this high-mindedness was perhaps excessive had never occurred to him.

"Lord Rossmere."

Until her voice broke into his thoughts, he hadn't noticed Lady Jane seated on a stone bench at the joining of two paths. Coming on her suddenly this way after his godmother's suggestion, he took in her appearance with fresh eyes. The most impressive thing about her was her height, which gave her an unconscious elegance. Though her features were less than classical, she had humorous hazel eyes and a warm smile. There was nothing unique about her brown hair, which she wore braided and wound around the crown of her head for this hot summer day. An attractive woman, but nothing out of the ordinary.

"Lady Jane. Forgive me for being so oblivious. May I join you?"

"Certainly." She tucked her skirts in under her to make room for him on the bench. "You've been talking with Mabel," she suggested.

"How did you know? Does one wear an especially stricken look after being with your aunt?"

Jane laughed. "No, it was your survey of me which

23

gave you away." She waved a hand to dismiss any apology on his part. "I daresay she approached you with her unrealistic plan. She offered it to me earlier, you see. I told her she should abandon her efforts, but I know her better than to believe she would."

Rossmere's reply was cautious. "I realize her intentions are for the best. She has been remarkably kind to me over the last few years and I would hesitate to cause her any distress, but her scheme seems, as you say, unrealistic."

"Totally impractical. For my part, I have no intention of marrying."

"Nor I."

"Excellent. Then we shan't find it necessary to discuss the matter further." Jane's mischievous smile made a dimple appear in her cheek. "I would be perfectly willing to be the one to pass on the bad news to her."

"Perhaps you shouldn't do it immediately," Rossmere said, remembering the promise he'd made. "She'll be more accepting of our decision if we spend a little time together and then assure her that we wouldn't suit."

Jane lifted her shoulders in a slight shrug. "As you wish. I've always found it best to be entirely forthright with Aunt Mabel, else she's likely to press her advantage."

"I thought we might ride out together tomorrow or drive into the village, something that would indicate our making an effort."

"I'd prefer driving to the village, I think. Ascot might make my mare a bit skittish. She's young and we haven't had her long."

Another of them objecting to Ascot, he thought with a touch of annoyance. Driving would mean his having to borrow a curricle from Lord Barlow, as he hadn't one of his own. Still, he refused to retract the invitation. "In the morning, perhaps? Say, ten o'clock?"

"That would be fine." Jane rose from the stone bench and patted out her skirts. Rossmere heard the rustle of a piece of paper in her pocket. Jane's long, thin fingers drew a letter partially out and she asked, "Do you know the Ashwickes, Lord Rossmere?"

It took him a moment to place the name. "Cranford, of course. From Westmoreland, isn't it?"

"Yes. He's married now and his wife has written to say they have a baby boy. Odd, how these things work out," she mused. "When I first met her, she thought he was intolerably stuffy, and he thought she was a hopeless imp. Whereas, Nancy . . ." She stopped abruptly and jammed the letter back into her pocket. "Forgive me. My mind was wandering. Until dinner, Lord Rossmere."

He dipped his head in a gesture of acknowledgment, but his eyes had become wary. What had been the point of those strange remarks? It was almost as if she'd forgotten to whom she was speaking for a moment. He frowned after her as she walked away from him.

Her graceful carriage drew his notice. To his surprise he discovered that Lady Jane had a fully developed figure that was quite pleasing to the eye. He had failed to remark it previously because he had paid so little heed to her. He decided, with a rueful shake of his head, that he wouldn't make the same mistake in the future. If he was going to spend some time in her company, he might as well derive what enjoyment he could from the experience.

3

Jane's father, Lord Barlow, was subject to attacks of gout. She was accustomed to accompanying him to Bath now and again, where the waters did something to aid him, but not as much as the company they found there. At fifty-five the earl was still active when the gout wasn't bothering him, and his mind was always alert to his favorite subject, the antiquities of Greece and Rome. Jane's own fascination with these ancient treasures had been generated by his, and was almost as strong.

Willow End was a repository of actual artifacts from the old civilizations, as well as of reproductions of Lord Barlow's favorite statues. Few of them were without their missing arms or legs, and Rossmere, unaware of the seriousness with which such matters were viewed in the household, had one night remarked that the ones in the gold drawing room were "quite a motley crew."

Lord Barlow had blinked at him and cleared his throat before remarking that their incompleteness was a circumstance of their antiquity.

Still not catching on to the significance of the older man's darkening countenance, Rossmere chuckled. "Ancient amputees," he said. "Very colorful."

26

Lord Barlow had looked almost apoplectic. Jane had had to bite her lip to keep from entering the fray. Fortunately Mabel knew how to change a subject so deftly that neither Lord Barlow nor the viscount was aware precisely how they found themselves discussing Italian marble. But Lord Barlow had remarked later to Jane, with some chagrin, "The young fool hasn't the first idea how rare and valuable my collection is. If he knew that any one of these statues would pay his mortgage for a quarter, he'd probably slit his wrists!"

The earl had, over the years, trusted his curricle to any number of young men, but on this occasion, perhaps because of Rossmere's ignorance of matters antiquarian, he supervised the harnessing of his pair and waited to see if the viscount proved to be an adequate whipster. Jane couldn't imagine what he intended to do if Rossmere exhibited two left hands in the matter. Surely he wouldn't bellow after them to return to the stables, as he had with his own misbehaving children.

It was obvious to Jane that Rossmere disliked this kind of unwarranted supervision. He stood rigid beside the gleaming black vehicle with its red wheels and gold crest, returning polite but brief answers to the leading questions Lord Barlow threw at him. "And what would you do if the curricle overturned on you?" the earl demanded.

"I would probably expire on the spot."

Jane laughed and patted her father's cheek. "Have you seen him in the saddle, Papa? Anyone who can ride that well is bound to be more than adequate as a driver."

"Just look at the horse he rides," Lord Barlow muttered. "Oh, very well. Off with you, then."

Rossmere set the horses at an easy pace down the avenue of willow trees. It was a cooler day than the previous one and Jane watched the elegant tendrils dance in the warm breeze. As a child she had spent long hours under those branches, her chin propped on her hands and her mind filled with the glories of whatever book she was reading. She wondered now why she hadn't taken a book there in so many years.

The village of Lockley was only a mile distant. More often than not she walked the short distance, but she was content to share the curricle with him. It was hard to tell if he really was a good driver because the road was undemanding: wide, straight, and untraveled by any other vehicle. She suspected that he could drive to an inch.

"Papa wouldn't have questioned your driving ability, Lord Rossmere, except for your remarks on his antiquities. I have to tell you that he questions the competence of anyone who doesn't understand his consuming passion for them."

"But surely there are very few who do."

"More than you'd suppose, but still, not many," she admitted.

"Do you share it?"

"Oh, yes. Though I'm the only one of his children who does. A great disappointment to him, Samuel and Geoffrey not taking after him in that respect. He doesn't care so much about Margaret or Nancy."

"Your brothers and sisters don't live in the area anymore, do they?"

"Nancy does. The Parnham estate is three miles the other side of Lockley, so we see her now and again." A tiny frown drew down her brow. "Not as often as I should like, of course. I'm very fond of Nancy. She's eight years younger and I feel I helped to raise her. Now she has a baby of her own."

"Parnham." Rossmere seemed to be searching his mind for some connection to the name. After a moment he shrugged. "Your father's pair is extremely well-matched for appearance and gait. I used to have chestnuts very like them. It's been a while since I've driven anything more demanding than a farm cart," he said, eyeing her challengingly.

"I daresay that takes even more skill than a curricle,

all things considered. Aunt Mabel told me you're determined to make the farming profitable enough to bail out Longborough Park."

"It will take years, but the land is good and my tenants are hard workers."

This seemed a propitious moment to bring up the matter of Graywood, but how? Jane glanced at Rossmere's profile with its firm chin and aristocratic nose. A proud man. Every feature indicated it, as did his inflexible bearing. The references to his financial straits were warnings to her rather than confidences. It was as though he were saying, "You know where I stand, and I know you know it, but you'll never prove that it distresses me unduly." Obviously she would have to be blunt.

"If Richard had died intestate, you would have inherited Graywood and the rest of his property."

His jaw tightened. "But he didn't die intestate."

"No, he left a will. An old will. A will made after his first episode of . . . madness."

"I'm sure it was none the less valid for that."

"Are you?"

He didn't even bother to meet her interested gaze. "Quite sure."

"You would have benefited more from his inheritance than I did. If he'd known he was going to die so young, perhaps he'd have disposed of his property in a completely different manner."

"I doubt it. He wanted you to have it, Lady Jane. That's perfectly understandable. He would have married you if he could."

"And Graywood would have gone to our children, not to me. There would have been a comfortable jointure for me, an arrangement for a dower house, but the estate itself would have been passed on to the next generation."

"I don't take your point, ma'am."

"The property would have been passed on to family, to those deserving of it." They were nearing the village and

Jane laid a hand on his arm to draw his attention. "If I'd known he was going to die and I'd been more aware of your . . . situation, I would have insisted that he leave Graywood to you."

His cool eyes met her steady gaze. "Commendable, I'm sure, Lady Jane, but there's no need for you to offer this explanation. What's done is done."

"That's what I'm trying to tell you, in this awkward manner, Lord Rossmere. That what is done does not necessarily have to stay done in this particular way. Graywood itself I could not possibly part with, but the estate generates a great deal of revenue that is not needed to see to its upkeep. I think that revenue would best be diverted to Longborough Park. Richard would have been pleased with such an arrangement."

"Well, I wouldn't!" His voice grated through clenched teeth and his silver-blue eyes glinted with an icy anger. "My godmother's generosity is quite enough for me to accept. I don't wish yours or anyone else's. I beg your pardon if that sounds rude, Lady Jane, but I personally find it most disagreeable for other people to concern themselves so closely with my affairs."

"I daresay," Jane returned. "To be perfectly frank, Lord Rossmere, I'm not particularly concerned with your affairs, nor with your difficult straits. I am, however, concerned with disposing of Richard's property in a way that will leave my conscience clear. Now that the matter has been brought to my attention, I think it would benefit us both if you were to temper your pride with a little practicality and come to some agreement with me."

"I won't hear another word on the subject."

Jane laughed. "You sound like a poor, defenseless maiden whose virtue has been assaulted, my dear Rossmere. Spare me your self-defeating pretension. If there's one thing that distresses me in a man, it's this kind of odious, self-indulgent pride."

"What the devil would you know about a man's pride

and whether it's self-indulgent?" his lordship demanded. They were on the main (and only) street of the village, and he drew the horses to a stop in front of a greengrocer's shop. He made no attempt, however, to descend from the curricle, but sat glaring at her, the reins held tightly in his hands.

"It may surprise you," she said, her usual calm undisturbed, "but I know a great deal about pride, and men, and self-indulgence. I've had the opportunity of being an observer in society for many years now. I take a great interest in human nature."

"Do you?" He made no attempt to restrain the sarcasm in his voice. "No doubt you have vast experience on which to base your judgments. A maiden woman from a privileged family, gleaning tidbits of scurrilous information about her contemporaries. I don't think you could possibly have the first idea of 'human nature,' Lady Jane."

"Scurrilous information, indeed!" she retorted. "Don't try to twist my words, Rossmere. My knowledge comes from my ability to empathize with my fellow beings, not to judge them."

"And what do you call terming me self-indulgent?"

"It's no more than the truth, is it? You would rather see a fine old estate dwindle into rack and ruin than accept assistance from a well-meaning friend. What do you think I'd do if you took the money? Spend my time reminding you of my generosity? Is being a viscount without a penny to his name all that demanding a situation that it claims all your pride?"

He allowed the greengrocer's boy to tie his pair to a post, but turned to her before he climbed down. "Perhaps it is. You have no idea how it feels to lack sufficient funds for your daily expenses."

"But I can imagine it. I have an excellent imagination, and a heart that's suffered pain to guide me. You reject the humiliation of your situation, pretending it is no more than an inconvenience. Balderdash! It rules your life. Anyone can see that. Only you are too blind and too proud to acknowledge it and accept help!"

"Spare me from women who think they understand the first thing about men! They do nothing but indulge their own flights of fancy when they analyze some poor devil and pronounce him a saint or a sinner. The whole thing is a product of the gothic novels they read, and just about as reliable as a source of truth."

At this point in their exchange they were interrupted by the sound of a delighted laugh across the street. Jane turned to see a woman observing them with great amusement. The woman had flaming red hair and wore a charming emerald-green walking dress. Her abigail carried a variety of packages from the dressmaker's shop they had obviously just left.

"Why, Rossmere," the woman exclaimed, "I had no idea you could be so uncivil as to argue with a lady!" Her eyes were shining with merriment, and a smile played temptingly around her mouth, never quite settling.

The viscount stared at her, allowing an awkward moment to pass before he turned to his companion. "Do you know Mrs. Madeline Fulton, Lady Jane?"

"I had heard someone of the name took the Bentwick cottage. How do you do?" She remained perched on the curricle seat, because her hand was suddenly, and firmly, planted to it by Lord Rossmere. Assuming that this meant she wasn't to have a closer acquaintance with the woman, Jane assessed her with a lively curiosity. It wasn't every day that such a situation arose in sleepy Lockley.

Mrs. Fulton inclined her head. "It's a pleasure to meet you, Lady Jane. I've indeed taken the Bentwick cottage. A charming house, with a lovely prospect of the surrounding countryside. I'm told that Willow End is just beyond my view, but that it is the loveliest place in the county."

Rossmere interposed to prevent Jane from engaging in

THE PROUD VISCOUNT

a polite rejoinder. "Lord Barlow's seat is certainly an impressive one. But please, don't let us delay you, Mrs. Fulton. Your abigail is already staggering under the weight of all those packages. I hope your stay in Lockley will be a pleasant one."

With a smile of wry amusement, Mrs. Fulton thanked him, nodded to Jane, and walked off. Jane thought it rather a saucy walk, as if the woman had perfectly understood that he was trying to prevent any further contact between them and that she found this altogether too priggish of him. So far as Jane knew from local sources, Mrs. Fulton was accepted in the town as a widow, and a very attractive one. No hint of anything compromising had reached her ears.

But the choice of the Bentwick cottage was rather interesting. It stood at the edge of town in a little wood, so that a visitor not wishing to be noticed could hide his horse in the trees and enter quite unnoticed by the villagers through the back door. The perfect spot, in fact, for a rendezvous.

Jane allowed Rossmere to hand her down from the carriage, asking, "How is it you know Mrs. Fulton, Lord Rossmere?"

"I was acquainted with her in London," he replied. "Have you a list? Which of the shops did you wish to visit first?"

"So you think she's not someone with whom I should be acquainted, is that it? A charming-looking woman. And with a sense of humor, I would say. She wasn't at all put out by your brusqueness. Do you know, I had the impression she knew you rather well."

"I will not discuss her, Lady Jane."

"My, my, what a lot of subjects you refuse to discuss," she said. "I shall have to make a list of them and keep it to hand so as not to annoy you in future."

"Let's try the greengrocer's first. I'm sure your cook has made a request for something here." Rossmere put an insistent hand on her elbow and guided her toward the door.

"Plums and greengages. Everything else the gardener grows in the gardens or the conservatory. Cook wants to make a greengage tart and a vol-au-vent of plums. Of course, if you'd prefer a raspberry-and-currant tart . . ."

"Greengage will be fine."

"Saturday we're having my sister and her husband to dine with us. And Papa has invited some former neighbors. Aunt Mabel is determined to have roast grouse and curried lobster. Are you fond of cards? Mr. Parnham is especially good at whist. Well, I should say he's quite a hand at faro and hazard when the opportunity arises, but my father prefers simpler games at home."

Jane continued in this vein before the greengrocer and his lad as she inspected the bins of fruits and vegetables. She only glanced at the viscount rather absently when she asked her innocuous question. Yet his face took on a sharp, wary look. "Oh, dear. Another subject I mustn't discuss. What is it this time, Lord Rossmere? Gambling? Card games? Roast grouse? Curried lobster? Pray tell me."

He stared at her, uncomprehending. Then his gaze swept to the window, where he appeared to search for something. There was nothing in the street except the curricle and pair. No villagers strolled past and no other horses or carriages descended on the scene. With a frown he brought his gaze back to her. "I beg your pardon. Did you ask me something?"

"Are you quite well?" she asked, concerned. "Perhaps a touch of heat . . ."

"Nonsense! My attention was merely distracted for a moment."

She had seen nothing to distract it and found his behavior oddly suspicious, but she wasn't going to argue with him. "I merely wondered if you enjoyed playing whist. We frequently have a few hands when my sister comes to dine."

"I'm tolerably fond of it."

"Fine. We offer music, too, of course. Nancy plays quite well and we've always sung together, as a family. Do you think this plum is ripe enough? Cook plans to use it today."

They visited three other shops during the next hour and she managed to elicit from Lord Rossmere the information that he liked salmon and detested high-crowned women's hats, that he thought every house needed a brass door knocker and that no house needed a cute spinning wheel in the parlor. Though his mind seemed to wander occasionally, he obviously made an effort to follow Jane's conversation and add his contribution to it. Not until they were driving back to Willow End did he put forward any topic of his own.

"How long has your sister Nancy been married to Mr. Parnham?"

The question sounded innocent enough. Too innocent, to Jane's mind. "Almost a year and a half. Their son was born in March."

"I see. And she's how old?"

"Twenty last month. Were you trying to figure out how ancient *I* am?" she asked with an impudent grin.

But he looked surprised. "No. I'm quite aware that you are twenty-eight, Lady Jane. Your aunt referred to it as an age of genteel maturity. An interesting term. Do you suppose she thinks it ungenteel to be older, or younger, or both?"

"She thinks it is the perfect age for me to marry, since it is the age I've acquired. Poor Aunt Mabel. She must have minded being a spinster more than we've ever imagined. I shan't mind it at all."

"How can you possibly know that?"

"I know it instinctively. The way you know that you

could not bear to be under an obligation to me," she added, her eyes shining in the noonday sun.

"And here I was under the impression that you were a woman of genteel maturity, with polished manners and elegant conversation. My godmother never let on that your tongue had a sting to it."

"I daresay she's never noticed. I'm not moved to use it all that often."

"Should I count myself fortunate that I've inspired you?" he asked. For the first time a touch of humor lightened his voice.

"You may if you wish."

Jane leaned back against the plush upholstery of the carriage and studied him with thoughtful eyes. Decidedly a handsome man, but too proud and too cold to win her approval. Richard had been such an agreeable man, warm and generous. Rossmere could not compete with his memory in any way.

But she intended to spend a certain amount of time with the viscount. His behavior in the greengrocer's shop had been decidedly intriguing. Lady Jane had gotten the distinct impression that he knew something she really ought to learn. And she had every intention of finding out what it was.

4

On Saturday Jane felt restless. Nancy and John Parnham were due to arrive in late morning and spend the day at Willow End. But her sister's husband was given to last-minute changes of plan. When they hadn't arrived by noon, Jane feared this would be another occasion on which there would be a message sent about a mysterious indisposition, or a fear for a change in the perfect weather, or a misunderstanding as to the time and day. Jane was pacing the flower beds on the north side of the house when Rossmere came upon her.

"Out for a breath of air?" he asked.

"Yes. Even the summer parlor gets stuffy in this kind of heat."

"I thought your sister was expected this morning."

"She is. I still have hopes that they are merely late. Certain people always manage to be delayed by an endless stream of interruptions. Have you ever noticed that?"

"I suppose so. Would you care to ride for a while?"

"Oh, I couldn't when they might arrive at any moment." Jane cocked her head toward the drive and smiled with relief. "I believe I hear a carriage now."

"Perfect timing," he murmured. "You must get over

this alarm about Ascot, you know. He's reasonably well-behaved and wouldn't give your mare the least fright."

"Another time, perhaps," she replied as she hastened toward the carriage drive. "I should be there to welcome them."

Jane rounded the corner of the house in time to see the Parnham carriage rolling up the willow avenue. The fact that it was a new carriage made her bite her lip. How extravagant the man was! They had a perfectly adequate carriage for the small amount of travel about the district that they undertook. Jane shrugged off her annoyance as the coachman drew the team to a halt directly in front of the portico.

Hardly able to wait for a footman to open the door and let down the steps, Nancy waved excitedly to her sister from within. She was handed down with a dignity that did not match her own hurried enthusiasm. "Oh, it's so good to see you, Jane! It's entirely my fault that we're late, so you must forgive me. And will you look at the baby? He's grown so much since you've seen him, you'll hardly recognize him."

The nursemaid, a girl of perhaps sixteen, sat with the sleepy baby in her lap. John Parnham had climbed down after his wife. He didn't turn to observe the baby, as everyone else was doing, but spoke to his father-in-law as the latter came down the front stairs. "Your grandson is going to be a bruising rider, Lord Barlow. You can tell it already."

The earl smiled. "He'll certainly have every encouragement, I'm sure. How do you do, John?"

"Very well, sir. I can see you're in remarkable health, yourself. What do you think of the new carriage?"

Lord Barlow made the required comments on the design and appearance of the landau, though Jane had noticed that it was made up, in the royal style, with rear seating for two carriage footmen. Surely a great pretension for the Parnham family, whose fortunes had been running a little low when Nancy's dowry provided a welcome infusion. Again Jane shrugged off her annoyance. She was not going to let such a small matter spoil her chance to have an enjoyable visit with her sister.

Rossmere had moved around the house at a leisurely pace and now joined the group on the gravel drive. John Parnham acknowledged the meeting with an elegant bow, his wife with a charming curtsy. Jane found the contrast between the two men quite striking.

Parnham was the more handsome, by current standards. He had blond hair cut in the Brutus style, and eyes of a neutral shade of brown. His features were classical, but in a different way than Rossmere's. The viscount's nose, chin, and cheekbones were aggressive while Parnham's were softer, smoothed out like those of a statue weathered over the years. Nancy's husband never dressed in anything less than the latest style; Rossmere's clothing had the mark of country tailoring, good quality but less than the height of fashion.

John Parnham was an affable man. From the beginning of his acquaintance with the family at Willow End, he had put himself out to charm them. His countenance was open and his speech unreserved. If he tended to be extravagant in his expenditures, well, it cost a pretty penny to be fashionable these days and it was important to him to be fashionable. He had once, at Jane's slight frown, teased her by saying, "You wouldn't want your sister married into a shabby establishment, now would you?" It did seem to Jane, though, that there must be more pressing matters than a new carriage that laid claim to his pocketbook.

Rossmere was another type of man altogether. He made an effort to be civil, but no attempt to win the affections of those around him. His reserve was almost chilling, and his pride gave him a faintly superior air. And he was stubborn, Jane added mentally. Another contrast with the accommodating John Parnham.

Parnham was the first to claim prior knowledge. "We met years ago," he said, regarding the viscount with an amiable smile. "Perhaps you will have forgotten. It's been a long time."

"I haven't forgotten," Rossmere admitted without a matching enthusiasm. "I had no idea you were from this part of the country."

"Only recently. Fire destroyed the family estate a few years back and it gave me the opportunity to search out a more congenial area. I was fortunate indeed to settle so close to Willow End."

"Weren't you?" Rossmere allowed his gaze to rest on Nancy, the youngest of the Reedness children. She was considerably shorter than her sister, and plump. This might have been the effect of having recently carried a child, but the viscount thought not. She had the general carriage of a normally plump girl. It surprised Rossmere that such a fashionable blade as Parnham would ally himself with a dumpling of a female. As often as not, the blades considered girls of her appearance quite beneath their notice.

And yet Nancy was a lovely woman. Her creamy complexion and warm eyes combined to make her look fresh with the promise of a spring morning. Not innocent precisely, but Rossmere guessed that hers was a trusting nature, confiding, candid. Her husband's energetic camaraderie seemed almost gauche when set next to Nancy's subdued charm. The viscount watched as Jane and Nancy linked arms and climbed the stairs to the house, with the nursemaid trailing behind.

"Of course, most people would have rebuilt in Yorkshire," Parnham continued. "I tried to be a bit more farsighted than that. What was the sense of putting up a modern structure when elsewhere I could purchase something with a bit of history to it? And the weather is so foul in Yorkshire. Always dismal. Since I was the last of the family, I had the chance to please only myself with where I settled. Sussex is such fine country, and so close to London."

"Indeed. Do you go there often?" Rossmere asked.

Parnham flipped a negligent hand outward. "Occasionally. On business, you understand. It's convenient being able to conduct matters for myself rather than having to employ an agent. I've even been of use to Lord Barlow once or twice."

The earl nodded acknowledgment. "I don't like going to London these days if I can help it," he confessed to Rossmere. "Entirely too crowded there. The only thing that draws me at all is the Elgin Marbles."

Rossmere thought Parnham winked at him at this point in the conversation. Really, unless the man had gotten a speck of dirt in his eye, he had actually had the effrontery to offer a conspiratorial wink to a man he scarcely knew! Making fun of the old man's passion for broken statues, was what he was about. Though Rossmere cherished some sentiments on the same order, he was annoyed by Parnham's behavior, for no reason that he could quite put a finger on. Perhaps he simply didn't like Parnham, something that had occurred to him within minutes of meeting the young jackanapes again.

"I never see you there anymore," Parnham mentioned.

Because he had lost the thread of their discussion, Rossmere had to think a moment before replying. "I haven't been to London in two years."

"Lost your taste for it, have you?"

The question, so lightly asked, seemed to Rossmere to contain a barb. The viscount very much feared it had either to do with women (and with Mrs. Madeline Fulton in particular) or to do with his own lack of financial resources (and being unable to afford the expensive capital). In either case, Parnham had only managed to raise his hackles higher. Rossmere chose not to answer the question.

Parnham didn't appear to notice. He spoke of his new

carriage and the likelihood of a spectacular harvest. After Parnham's wink, Rossmere was surprised to see the fellow actually pull a book about antiquities from his pocket and hand it to Lord Barlow. "I understand Thorson touches on some interesting elements of the baths," he said, sounding almost knowledgeable. "Thought you might like to see it."

"I was about to send for it!" the earl exclaimed. "Good of you to go to the trouble, Parnham. Very good indeed."

The young dandy obviously knew how to please his father-in-law, Rossmere decided. He tried, for a moment, to believe that it really *was* good of Parnham to go to the bother of searching out the right book for the older man. But it struck him more as toadying and he dismissed Parnham as an apple-polisher. Rossmere felt sure no one would find him trying to win the earl's approval by such means if he were married to one of Barlow's daughters.

Irritated beyond reason, Rossmere dropped a little behind the other two men, hoping it would not be necessary for him to spend the whole day with John Parnham.

In the sitting room off Jane's bedroom Nancy had the nursemaid put the child down on a blanket. The corner room caught a good cross-breeze and stayed relatively cool in the warm weather. Nancy dismissed the girl, sending her down to the kitchen for a glass of lemonade and saying she would send for her when she needed her. Then she turned to Jane with a smile.

"I was so afraid something would arise to prevent our coming. How I would have hated not seeing you! It's been too long." She gave her sister a hug and seated herself in a chair beside little William. "The baby's beginning to creep now. See how he gets on his hands and knees and rocks like that? I think it's the most amusing thing."

Jane seated herself on the floor beside her nephew.

"What a clever lad he is. Do you think he has John's nose?"

"Absolutely. And his hair and his eyes. I think perhaps he'll have John's disposition, too. He's very cheerful and ready to try a new adventure at the drop of a pin."

The baby gurgled and rocked so hard that he tumbled over on the blanket. He looked surprised and his little mouth puckered up in preparation for a wail of protest, but Jane distracted him with her pocket watch. His eyes shone with interest and he reached for the swinging gold timepiece. When he had it safely in hand, he carried it to his mouth to taste.

"No, no," Jane protested. "This one is only for looking at. Have you something he can gum?"

Nancy withdrew a crust from her pocket. "I always carry something with me. John says I've begun to shed bread crumbs." She handed the crust to William, saying, "Tell me about Lord Rossmere. Has he been good company for you?"

Jane laughed. "Aunt Mabel is scheming to marry us off. It was her sole intent in inviting him here, I gather. But neither of us is interested."

"How ungallant of him to let you know that!"

"Oh, he didn't precisely say it, but it is very clear. Mabel believes he needs a rich wife, and she seems to think I'll be a miserable spinster one day if I pass up this opportunity."

"And don't you think you will?"

"No, dear, I don't. Can you imagine me miserable?"

"No, but I can picture you happily married. I just don't know that Lord Rossmere is the man for you. He seems rather stiff and uncompromising."

"Hmmm. Perhaps. It's hard to tell. You should see him on Ascot."

"He brought the horse?" Nancy asked in disbelief.

"It doesn't seem to have occurred to him that it would disturb anyone."

"Men live in the most blinkered world, don't they? John thinks nothing of disappearing for days on end without telling me where he's going, and he's offended if I ask him where he's been on his return. How very uninterested they must think women are in what goes on about them in the world."

This was the first time Nancy had confided any such behavior to her sister. Jane didn't want to frighten off any further confidences by making too much of it. She was distressed to hear such a tale, but she remained calm. "That is indeed too bad of him. But let me tell you what happened in the village yesterday." Jane proceeded to tell her about Mrs. Fulton, taking Rossmere to task for leaving the incident unresolved.

Her sister frowned. "A redheaded woman? Quite slender and beautiful? Yes, I've seen her there. She doesn't seem like someone who would live secluded in Lockley, does she?"

"Certainly not! And the worst of it was that I'm quite sure Rossmere has had some connection with her. She spoke so familiarly to him. Actually," she admitted, her eyes twinkling, "his discomfort was just the least bit amusing, because he's so stuffy sometimes."

"You mean you think she was his mistress?" Nancy asked, her eyes wide with astonishment.

"I wouldn't be surprised. He was quite the metropolitan gentleman, I'm told, before his father brought on their ruin."

"He's a good-looking man, in a rugged sort of way. I remember once when he visited Richard, and I was perhaps fifteen. I had quite a *tendre* for him. Naturally he didn't notice me at all. To him I was a child."

"He has a way of treating women like children, I think. There's a polite distance, a tolerance for the less-advantaged, about the way he speaks with me. And though he's very respectful to Aunt Mabel, he treats her much the same way."

"Hmm. Men must think women have a lesser intelligence when really it is only the disparity in education. Sometimes John's attitude forces me to expedients that I deplore. I would far rather deal honestly with him than try to maneuver him into doing what I want."

"I'm afraid I don't follow you," said Jane, fearing very much that she did.

"I shall give you an instance. John didn't really wish to come for this visit. I was fearful that he would cancel it at the last moment, but I knew how much he likes to earn Papa's good esteem. So I sent off to Guildford for a book on antiquities I'd read of that I thought Papa would particularly enjoy. When it arrived, very fortuitously, yesterday afternoon, I told John that the book he'd suggested getting for Papa had come in time for our visit."

"Surely he knew he'd never said any such thing."

"Not really. When I ran across the original reference to the book, I read it aloud to him. In situations of that sort it's never clear who said that it was something Papa would like. And who is going to remember whether we actually determined to purchase it for him?"

"Good heavens! It sounds a very complicated way to deal with a husband."

Nancy shrugged and studied the gold wedding band on her finger. "It wouldn't be my preferred method, Jane, I assure you. But my opinions don't seem to hold much weight with him in the ordinary course of things, and I am driven to this subterfuge."

"Well, you have only been married a short time," her sister offered by way of reassurance. "Once he learns what a fine, practical intelligence you possess, I daresay he will make a point of consulting you."

Nancy said nothing, but dropped her gaze to little William, who was making tentative movements on his hands and knees.

*　　*　　*

Later that evening, when Jane was on her way to bed, Lord Rossmere overtook her in the first-floor corridor of the east wing. The candles flickered softly in their sconces on the walls, shedding a little light on the dark hall. Jane was tired and vaguely disturbed. At first she did no more than acknowledge the viscount's greeting with a nod and a slight smile. As he passed by, a thought occurred to her.

"Stay a moment," she called. "There was something I wished to ask you."

Only then did she notice that he'd already eased his neckcloth away from his throat so that his shirtpoints hovered ludicrously around his ears. Jane bit her lip to suppress a grin.

"What was it?" he asked rather brusquely.

"Did Mr. Parnham bring a book for my father today?"

"A book? Oh, yes. He had it in his pocket. Something about Lord Barlow's favorite subject, I believe."

"And he indicated that it was his own idea to acquire the book?"

"I don't quite understand what you're getting at, Lady Jane."

"Did he say it was from him, or from Nancy, or both of them?"

A flicker of annoyance appeared in Rossmere's eyes. "What difference could it possibly make? I don't remember. Though I'm fairly certain that he said he'd gotten it for your father. There was no mention of your sister."

Jane nodded. "Yes. Thank you. I fancied as much. It's what comes of having very little regard for another's opinion, you know, this convoluted behavior. Well, good night, Lord Rossmere."

He stared at her for a moment, then offered a curt nod and stalked off down the hall.

5

Lady Jane hated to see her sister leave in the morning, but Parnham was insistent that they had to return to Parnham Hall. The estate had been called Marsden Hall for so many years that the natives found it impossible to adapt to the new nomenclature, but Parnham corrected anyone who reverted to the old name. "After all," he was fond of saying, "the Marsden line has disappeared, and the Parnham line needs encouragement."

When the sparkling carriage was no more than a cloud of dust on the road, Jane wandered over to the willow trees and curled up under one as she had promised herself she would. The dew had burned off the grass and it smelled warmly fragrant. Swaying branches caught the slight breeze and brushed against her lemon jaconet muslin dress. Aunt Mabel would have cautioned her against getting grass stains on it.

Nancy's revelations about her marriage had disturbed Jane. It was always more pleasant to think that one's favorite people were perfectly happy. On the other hand, perhaps her other sister, Margaret, was right that certain adjustments always had to be made when one lived with another person. That sounded very reasonable. And yet

. . . Parnham disappeared for days on end without giving
any explanation. Now, that was really uncalled for. Nancy
was not, after all, a servant in the household, who might
be kept in ignorance of the master's doings.

Her thoughts were so deeply engrossing that she failed
to notice the viscount arrive on the other side of the fall
of leafy branches. When she finally looked up, she found
him observing her with interest, unmoving, his feet in
black boots planted a little distance apart. Jane remained
seated. She almost wished she could flutter her hand at
him to go away.

"May I join you?" he asked.

It sounded like a rhetorical question to her. He scarcely
waited for her nod before parting the branches and low-
ering himself to the ground beside her. He wore buckskin breeches and a riding coat, a much more appropriate
outfit for lying on the ground than her own. And he did
lie on the ground, while she sat primly with her knees
bent and her skirts tucked decorously about her.

"I was hoping you would ride with me today," he said.

"Thank you, but I have a thousand things to do."

"I can see that."

"This is one of the things I have to do," she insisted.
"I have to spend a little time alone, planning menus and
considering which of the laundry maids to promote to
dairy maid, and whether the new footman is working out
satisfactorily. He's not learned to protect the lower part
of a topboot when he's working on the top with pumice
stone. Really, it's so elementary I can't believe he would
have to be reminded more than once."

Rossmere considered the matter with mock gravity. "I
tell you what. You can have him take the place of the
laundry maid you promote to dairy maid. It will keep
him employed and out of harm's way."

Jane tried to match his lighthearted tone. "You really
think the laundry is out of harm's way? He would only

manage to ruin all our linens, I daresay. Put blacking in the wash water or some such thing."

"How little faith you have! Which reminds me. What was that about Parnham and the book last night?"

"Oh, nothing to signify. You will note that Parnham takes an interest in my father's hobby, rather than speaking of amputated goddesses."

Her attempt to distract him was not totally successful. He regarded her with intent blue eyes. "Or perhaps it was his wife who remembered your father's passion while the husband took credit for his thoughtfulness."

"I'm certain it's a book that Papa will enjoy," was all she replied.

Rossmere rolled over on his back and locked his fingers over his flat stomach. He didn't look at Jane. Instead, his gaze was absent, up through the tree to the sky above. "Parnham said some rather interesting things about your sister yesterday when you women left us to our port."

"What sort of things?"

"He spoke of how unsettling childbearing was to a woman. Very kindly, you understand. He intimated that the stress of such an event was sometimes the occasion of a . . . mmm, shall we say a mild instability? Nothing to be particularly concerned about, he felt sure."

Jane clenched her teeth together to prevent herself from saying something truly disagreeable about her brother-in-law. After a while she was able to ask, "How had he come to that conclusion?"

"Several erratic things she had done, I gather. Let me see. He enumerated them, each time extravagantly excusing such a small but odd occurrence as the product of an overactive fancy. The first occasion he recounted was shortly after his son and heir was born. Nancy announced suddenly, when the infant was in full sight of her, that his hands were on backward. Which they weren't."

Jane recalled that Nancy herself had told her this story

months ago, as a sort of joke on herself and her fears that something would be wrong with the baby. It was an instance of anxiety and confusion that could easily happen to a woman so soon after lying in. Parnham, of course, might have viewed the matter differently.

"Then there was the time Parnham found her dressed to go out on an evening when there had been no invitation," Rossmere continued in an even, deep voice. "On that occasion Nancy insisted that indeed there had been a card, from the Cutfords, and that she had mentioned the matter to him. But she was unable to find any card, and by chance Mr. Cutford, Junior, happened to call in just at that time and Parnham discovered by discreet query that there was no invitation at all."

It was hard to know what to make of this tale. Nancy had never mentioned anything of the kind. Jane considered the various possible explanations and frowned. "Go on. What else did he say?"

"Though he indicated that there were several other instances of that general nature, he did not elaborate on them. He was much more concerned about a recent event that showed a deepening of her . . . distress. On this occasion, barely a week ago, her delusion was much more serious."

Jane could feel her heart hammering in her chest. Rossmere closed his eyes, as though trying to remember precisely how Parnham had told this particular story. His voice took on an almost disembodied quality.

"It was the stormy night, Monday, I think. Parnham had been into Lockley during the afternoon and on the way back his horse threw a shoe. He returned to Lockley and waited for the smith to repair it, which took an unconscionable amount of time, he said. When he got back to Parnham Hall, it was already dark and the storm had begun.

"I can't remember whether he said the servants didn't know where Mrs. Parnham was, or whether they thought

she was in her room. Parnham was soaking wet and went
directly up to change. While he was changing, he heard
noises coming from the balcony and then a feeble pounding on the door. He went immediately to open it, and
there was Nancy, soaking wet and sobbing."

Before she could stop herself, Jane snapped, "Nonsense!"

Ignoring this interruption, he continued. "According
to Parnham, she clung to him and begged to know why
he had locked her out on the balcony. Well, he was
never so flabbergasted. In the first place, he had only
just returned home, and in the second, the balcony door
wasn't locked!"

"I've never heard such a pack of lies."

"But, Lady Jane, his valet was just coming in with a
fresh shirt and heard the whole," Rossmere assured her
with a decided lack of conviction.

"What is the purpose of such a tale?"

Rossmere looked thoughtful. "He's a born storyteller,
of course, but I think this is more than an exaggeration.
Has your sister mentioned any of this?"

"Only the first one, about the hands being on backward. She was laughing at herself about that. I'm sure if
there were even a grain of truth to the others, she would
have said something. Does Parnham think this makes
him more acceptable in my father's eyes?"

"Your father is a little naïve, Lady Jane. He thinks of
women as rather a mystery, and he's not at all surprised
to hear tales of this sort. He was concerned, and coun-
seled Parnham to be sure that Nancy got plenty of rest
and didn't try to do too much."

"How could he be so taken in?" she demanded.

"As you say, what purpose could Parnham have for
lying?"

Jane found that his eyes were on her now. "Do you
believe him?"

"I don't know either of them well enough to make any

pronouncement. Fortunately it has nothing to do with me. I simply thought you should know, since your father strikes me as someone who won't bother to tell you, thinking the whole story a bit too upsetting for your fragile ears."

This forced a grin out of her. "You're very clever at determining what people are like, aren't you, Lord Rossmere?"

He rose from the ground and stood towering over her before answering. "Not always. I've had a few experiences that have taught me to pay a little closer attention." He held a hand down to her. "Would you like to go for that ride?"

Though she let him help her to her feet, she shook her head. "Really, I have things I have to attend to. You go right ahead."

"Very well. Perhaps another time."

"Perhaps."

Rossmere didn't like to leave her standing there alone under the giant willow tree. Though she maintained an outward calm, he could see that his information had distressed her. Her hazel eyes were troubled and the smooth line of her jaw was thrust minutely forward in anger or anxiety. She wasn't really seeing him, though her eyes followed as he turned away.

When he was about to round the corner of the stables, he looked back and found her still there, staring vacantly in his direction. He regretted having to burden her with this disturbing mystery, but her father apparently had no intention of unraveling it, and he himself hadn't the necessary knowledge. He had no doubt that Lady Jane was the one to approach. Her calm capability was her most obvious asset.

Not that she didn't have others. She was an elegant woman, with a lively mind and a sympathetic heart. And an income so vastly superior to his that he refused to think about it, or about her.

He gave instructions that Ascot be saddled. A good ride on that untamed beast would shake any unwelcome thoughts from his head. If there was one thing Lady Jane most certainly was not, it was untamed. She was civilized to within an inch of her life. In the best possible way, of course, but civilized nonetheless.

Rossmere was attracted to a less-restrained type of woman. Every lady of quality whom he'd ever met had struck him as impossibly reserved or ludicrously puffed up with her own consequence. In either case, these women had very little sparkle and absolutely no resplendence. Rossmere had grown up well-heeled, and he had developed a taste for the extravagant—in women, particularly.

And no woman he'd known had been as flamboyant, beautiful, and amusing as Madeline Fulton. He had met her when he was twenty-five and despairing of ever discovering a woman who truly embodied his desires. It was at the theater that he first caught a glimpse of her in a box across the way, her flaming hair catching the candle-light and her delicious laughter almost seeming to reach him. There were two other attractive women in the box, but she easily outshone them. Even at a distance her vitality couldn't be mistaken.

He had made a point of finding out who she was. Somewhat to his surprise, he learned that she was marginally accepted in society. This was occasioned by her being the widow of a war hero, rather than by her own birth. Her manner of living in London was suspect, but not reckless enough to be definitely censured. Rossmere never doubted for a moment that she was exactly the woman he wanted for his mistress.

Lord, the chase she had led him! He followed her to a succession of entertainments that were among the most interesting he'd ever attended, with their slight air of disreputability and their gay abandon. Madeline flirted outrageously with him at each of these balls, parties, breakfasts, routs, boating parties, but she refused to allow him to be alone with her. Her reputation was protected when he called on her by the presence of an elderly woman whom it took Rossmere several days to ascertain was stone-deaf. Later he had decided she didn't see all that well, either.

Madeline was the perfect temptress. She always let him know that she was interested, and yet she wouldn't allow him to come too close. Her dresses were low-cut and provocative, her smiles enticing and full of promise. When they waltzed together, Rossmere could hardly believe the satiny texture of her skin, the glowing warmth of her body. For these were not Almack's waltzes, but those dangerous, intoxicating dances held at the homes of her friends, where no eyebrow rose at the sight of two bodies so close together that they touched in any number of places rather than a decorous hand at the waist.

Ascot was brought to Rossmere and he swung up on the horse with practiced ease. The groom stepped warily around the huge animal, backing out of Ascot's way as soon as Rossmere indicated that he was settled. The viscount kept his horse on a tight rein until they were beyond the lawns. When he was given his head, Ascot surged into a gallop that had its usual effect of filling Rossmere with total abandon. Together they seemed to sail across the countryside at a remarkable pace, passing the fence posts and trees so quickly they almost blurred into one another.

It had been like that with Madeline. The thrill of the chase, the excitement of finally winning her as his mistress, the exotic nights in her bed—it had all blurred together into a time set apart from the rest of his life. She was everything he had ever looked for in a woman, and daily she delighted him with the proof of how perfectly she matched up with his dreams. What he imagined, she turned into reality.

Once he told her of a dream he'd had where a woman dressed only in a sheer muslin slip had ridden up to him on a white horse and held her hand out, beckoning him to follow her. He'd forgotten all about the dream when Madeline set an appointment to meet him in a secluded area of Richmond Park. He was there ahead of time, leaning against a tree, when he heard the soft sound of hoofbeats. They drew closer and he watched for the horse to emerge from the woods at a spot where there was no trail.

And there she was, her dazzling red hair flowing loose down over her shoulders, riding a white horse and wearing a wisp of material he could easily see through. She said nothing, but beckoned to him as she slowly guided the horse back into the trees. Mesmerized, he followed through the tangle of undergrowth, never losing sight of the horse and rider. Finally they came to a glade where a bower had been improvised. Madeline had already dismounted and lay on the waiting cushions. Rossmere joined her there, intoxicated by the living out of a fantasy.

Gradually she claimed a larger part of his thoughts until she became almost an obsession. He had never met anyone who was so adroit at accommodating his moods. She seemed to know him better than he knew himself. And she consequently became immensely important to him, a necessary part of his life. It was only a step to thoughts of marrying her.

Certainly she was not accepted into the inner circles of society, and never would be. But did he care? Wouldn't it be better to live a life filled with the kind of excitement she offered than to accept the stuffy existence his contemporaries wedged themselves into? This argument continually battled for supremacy in him, and it seemed, for a while, to be gaining ground.

It was a visit to Richard that had begun Rossmere's recovery. Though Richard was sturdily sane when not in the grip of his occasional madness, he had a sensitivity to disturbances in others that was almost uncanny. Before Rossmere had spent half a day with him, Richard said,

"You've allowed this woman to become an obsession, Stephen. You don't love her; you're consumed by her. Which tells me she's diabolically clever, since you're not ordinarily gullible."

Rossmere had at first indignantly ignored this wise counsel, and then he had argued against it. But his very resistance to the idea began to work its way into an understanding that there was something terribly wrong. Richard was relentless in making him trace the course of the association between Rossmere and Madeline. They sat for hours over glasses of small beer or Madeira, with Richard pointing out the steps by which he had been ensnared. Rossmere had hated every minute of it, like undergoing a particularly painful course of medical treatment. At the time it hadn't mattered that it was necessary for his health; it had simply hurt. But Richard insisted.

And then it was over. Knowing how a magician does his tricks may leave one with a respect for his skill, but it leaves one with no illusions about the authenticity of the tricks. Madeline was no longer a goddess. She was a clever woman, a genius as a seductress, but she was not the possessor of his heart. Rossmere learned from that experience, and one of the things he learned was that women were not to be trusted.

Shortly afterward, when his father gambled away the Rossmere fortune, he learned that it wasn't only women who weren't to be trusted.

Forced to become self-sufficient, he had also become a little cynical, but intrigued by the machinations of his fellow man. His curiosity had been aroused now by two very different circumstances at Willow End: John Parnham's unlikely tales of Nancy's behavior, and Madeline Fulton's presence in a village the size of Lockley. During the course of his month's promised stay at Willow End, he had every intention of finding out what was going on.

6

As always, the gallop on Ascot was a rewarding experience. When Rossmere had satisfied his need to feel unrestrained, he slowed the horse to a trot and headed for Lockley. It was only necessary to ask one person, a lad of ten or so, where the Bentwick cottage was located. In the country even the children knew where everyone lived.

The cottage sat at the edge of a small wood and slightly separated from the rest of the village. Everything about the place was well-maintained: the walk, the grass, the paint, the curtains in the windows. It looked wholly respectable, the dwelling of gentlefolk who would shop in the village shops and walk the length of the High Street nodding to their neighbors.

Rossmere never doubted that Madeline's rented home would be anything other than such a decorous cottage. He dismounted, tying Ascot's reins to an iron ring near the gate. The gravel walk had a flower border of roses and pansies, columbine and pinks. A flowering vine twisted up the side of the cottage and along the roofline. The air was fragrant with the perfume of sweet pea, a scent familiar to Rossmere from his boyhood at Longborough Park.

His knock at the door was answered by a fresh-faced girl wearing a maid's apron. He was surprised that Madeline would have a local girl privy to her secrets, but when the girl opened her mouth to speak, it was pure cockney that flowed from her tongue. Obviously Madeline had found this fresh-faced one in London.

" 'Ow can I help ya?" she asked.

Rossmere handed her his card, but the girl barely glanced at it. "I've come to call on Mrs. Fulton. Is she receiving?"

"I don't know as 'ow she is. 'Oo should I tell her is here?"

"Rossmere. I'm an old acquaintance of hers from London."

"Are you now?" The girl regarded him suspiciously. "I ain't never seed you before."

"Were you with her when she lived on the Edgeware Road?"

She didn't answer, but rubbed the card between her fingers. "Wait 'ere." She closed the door, leaving him on the stoop.

Rossmere studied the situation of the house. A very handy place, when one came to consider the matter. Anyone wishing to visit Madeline had no need to appear by way of the front door in sight of all the village residents. One could come over the Ridgely Road to the back of the tiny wood, tie one's horse to a tree inside the stand, and knock at the rear door (there always was one) without being seen by a soul. Very clever.

The maid reappeared and beckoned the viscount inside. There was a short hallway with several doors off it, plus a stairway leading above. Rossmere hesitated as the girl opened the first door on her right. "Mr. Rossmere," she announced carefully, if inaccurately.

"Do come in." Madeline stood by a writing desk, her hair piled lavishly on top of her head, with bright ringlets falling about her face. "I'd hoped you would call. Imagine meeting you in this part of the world, Rossmere."

"That's precisely what I thought," he said, lifting the hand she offered to his lips. "You look charming, as usual."

"How kind of you to say so." She waved him to the sofa and seated herself beside him. "It's been several years. You don't spend much time in London, I gather."

"As little as possible. Is Mrs. Smith no longer with you?"

"No. She's gone to live with her sister. In the country one can manage without a chaperone, I find. A few servants do much more nicely."

"Don't you miss London?"

"London is for the young and the rich," she temporized. "And I am neither."

"It's also for the beautiful," he replied with a gallantry he'd forgotten he possessed. "And you have beauty."

Madeline thanked him with a slight mocking smile. "Not to compare with the younger women, dear Rossmere. You forget that each year a new crop of desperately pretty girls arrives on the scene. A smart woman knows when to retire from the competition."

He didn't believe her for a minute. If she was in Lockley, it was not because she couldn't find a protector in London. There were few signs of aging on her lovely face, but it struck him suddenly that she must be of an age with Lady Jane. How very astonishing! And he had thought of the earl's daughter as quite old, for someone his godmother was pushing as a potential wife.

Madeline elaborated on her tale of retirement. "I have friends in the neighborhood. Oh, no one you would know, my dear fellow. Quite beneath your notice. And it is so much less expensive to live in the country; I'm sure you've found that yourself."

If this was a jab at his own poverty, he chose to ignore

it. "But there's so little to do here, for a woman of your . . . energies."

"Pooh! The delights of the countryside are underrated by those living dissipated lives in town. Think of the walks in the fresh air! The shopping at uncrowded stores in the High Street! The freshness of the fruits and vegetables! There's no limit to such pleasures."

Rossmerc laughed, as she had expected him to do. "And what if you wish to ride or drive? You don't appear to keep a carriage."

"There's a livery service at the inn on the Ridgely Road. I have only to send a message and a carriage arrives at my door. So much more sensible that housing a pair, with all their expense."

"But there are no masquerades, no breakfasts, no excursions to Astley's or Vauxhall. What do you do with yourself all day?"

"There are a thousand things to do," she said, dismissing his concern. "Reading and drawing and walking and eating. Really, there is scarcely time for everything I wish to accomplish. One wearies of the constant round of entertainments in the city. A little quiet seems more conducive to genuine happiness."

There was a suspicious twinkle deep in her green eyes, but she refused to be led by any avenue of conversation he attempted to explore. According to Madeline Fulton, she had settled here for the benefits of country living and she was more than happy with her choice. Certainly she looked content enough. One other possibility occurred to Rossmere.

"You're not *enceinte*, by chance?"

Her delighted laughter broke the quiet of the room. "With child? Oh, my dear, no. Whatever gave you that idea? As you can see, my figure is as slender as ever."

It was quite true, but rather discouraging, because Rossmere hadn't really learned a thing from her. He felt certain there was an important reason for her being in the country, and yet he couldn't learn the first thing about it. Whether she had had to leave London on the tail of some scandal (a duel? an embarrassing dismissal by a protector?), or had come to Lockley with a specific purpose, he was no closer to discovering.

He didn't dare stay longer. In a village the size of Lockley, there would be gossip if he failed to reappear and claim Ascot within a very short period of time. As he dismissed himself and wished her well, she said, "You must come again. But it's wise of you not to stay long. I have a reputation to protect here. Are you staying at Lord Barlow's seat?"

"Yes, my godmother is his-sister."

"Lady Jane is an attractive young woman. I'm surprised she's not married."

"I believe it is a matter of choice with her."

Madeline raised a brow. "Never believe such a thing, Rossmere. Marriage is a lady's only choice."

A rather odd thing for her to say, surely, he reflected as he bowed and strode from the cottage. Of course, he realized that she had hoped once that he would marry her, in spite of her tenuous position in society. All her clever planning had not been aimed at maintaining the extravagant allowance she received as his mistress. Her ultimate intention had been to convince him that she was more than just a mistress to him, that his own life was unorthodox enough not to be destroyed by making her his wife.

Had she some hope that sequestering herself in the country would lead to a permanent arrangement with some naïve country gentleman? There would be no one here to recollect her London reputation, no one to deny her account of her being the genteel widow of a war hero. Except himself. And his calling on her today might have set that fear to rest. That, or the knowledge that he wouldn't be around for long.

Ascot danced restlessly as Rossmere mounted. The

viscount allowed him his head again on their way back to Willow End. Even in the exhilaration of the ride, though, something nagged at his mind. Something about Madeline. Well, there was no sense in trying to grasp a wispy thought like that. It would come to him in time.

At the stables he dismounted and handed Ascot over to the wary groom. On the way to the house he passed no one and slipped through a rear door that took him to the entry hall by the least public corridor. Though he was anxious for some word from Longborough Park, he was in no mood to encounter any of the family just at present.

He found the post on the silver tray Winters always left on the mantel. There was, finally, a letter from Jim Wardy, the local man who had agreed to manage the estate in Rossmere's absence. Rossmere broke the seal and read the brief letter where he stood. Wardy was a man of few words: he needed Rossmere to send fifty pounds for unanticipated expenditures; otherwise all was fine on the estate and with the tenant farmers. It would have pleased Rossmere to hear of the progress of the crops, or the local gossip, but he had to content himself with what he'd received. And find a way to broach the subject of another loan pretty quickly to his godmother.

"Ah, there you are," Mabel said as she appeared suddenly across the hall from him. "Could I have a word with you?"

"I've just been riding Ascot and I fear I reek of the stables. I was on my way to change."

Mabel's nose twitched slightly. "Yes, indeed. Perhaps you'd have a moment before dinner. It's a matter of some importance."

Rossmere slipped the letter into his pocket with an inaudible sigh. "Of course. I could meet you in the north drawing room in half an hour."

"Excellent." Mabel dabbed unconsciously at her nose with a tiny lace handkerchief. "Such a nice day for a ride," she murmured as she turned away.

When he joined her later, she was frowning at a copy of the *Ladies' Magazine*. "I'm not at all certain it's a good thing that we're able to travel on the Continent again," she remarked. "So many astonishing things happen there."

"I daresay they think the same about us." He took a chair opposite her and arranged one long pantalooned leg over the other.

Mabel set the magazine aside and clasped her hands firmly in her lap. "I've noticed that you're spending some time with my niece, and I appreciate it. She's a delightful girl, isn't she?"

Rossmere would not have called her a girl, and he thought it was unwise of Mabel to do so, since it drew attention to just what an ungirlish age her niece had attained. "She's quite charming," he agreed.

"I knew the two of you would get along. From the very first, when the idea came to me, I felt you were absolutely destined for each other."

"My dear Lady Mabel, I'm afraid you're way ahead of us. Your niece and I have had several enjoyable exchanges, but we're hardly beyond the stage of new acquaintances. And I very much fear that there is a temperamental difference between us that could not be bridged."

"A temperamental difference?" Mabel was clearly disappointed. "What could that possibly be?"

Rossmere had no idea why he'd used that particular term. It had simply appeared on his tongue when the need for some excuse arose. There was no telling what harm could be done if Mabel were allowed to believe that things were progressing smoothly between him and Lady Jane. Faced with the necessity of explaining his words, he fell back on obscurity.

"Sometimes one is aware in getting to know another that there is a great difference between them. That is, one can have the highest regard for a person and yet feel the differences between them are too great to countenance any kind of ongoing alliance."

"Nonsense! You and Jane are ideally suited. Obviously you haven't gotten to know each other well enough yet to have discovered that." Mabel leaned toward him and tapped a bony finger on the back of his hand. "I'm an old hand at matchmaking. I directed each of Jane's brothers and sisters toward the right mate. Oh, there were plenty of possibilities of misalliances among them, but I persisted in urging them in the appropriate direction. And with Nancy . . . Well, that whole arrangement was mine from start to finish."

Astonished, but curious, Rossmere asked, "How did that come about?"

Mabel was clearly torn between pride in her accomplishment and the desire to get back to the more-pressing subject of their interview. Rossmere managed to look especially intrigued by her revelation, and she settled back slightly in her chair. "I understood John Parnham had only recently come to live in this area," he remarked by way of giving her a starting point.

"That's very true. His own estate, in Yorkshire or Westmoreland or some godforsaken spot, had burned to the ground. Not enough left to make it economical to rebuild on the same site, unless one was drawn to the area, and Mr. Parnham was not." She said this with some satisfaction. "So he scouted out the best possible location for his home and decided on our very neighborhood."

"Had he no relations to object to such a move? Usually there are three or four cousins determined to instruct one in the necessity of following tradition."

"If he has any relations, they are very distant ones. Mr. Parnham answers to no one save himself in such matters."

"I see. How very convenient for him!"

"It is very much the same for you," she reminded him severely. "Mr. Parnham bought an old manor house and furnished it in excellent taste. He made an effort to meet his neighbors and to support local businesses. Too often these old manor houses are bought by men who've grown rich in trade and haven't the first idea of how to behave in a country community such as ours. Mr. Parnham was a stroke of luck for Lockley. His manners are impeccable, he talks sensibly, he has wit, his person is pleasing—altogether a very agreeable man."

"And it was you who brought him to Lady Nancy's notice?"

Mabel disliked being rushed when she had settled into a tale. "Early on when he moved into the house, he came by and left his card. Jane and her father were in Bath at the time, and Nancy and I were in London for the Season, but due to return. Nancy had been successful in town, you understand, but she was never comfortable with the idea of marrying a stranger and disappearing off to his estate at some great distance, as Margaret had done."

"The youngest in a sizable family is often greatly attached to her home, I believe," Rossmere said.

"Sometimes. But Nancy is a biddable girl and would have adjusted to a different life if it had been necessary. Fortunately, when we returned from London, we became acquainted with Mr. Parnham almost immediately. Nancy was not taken with him at first. I daresay he seemed rather ordinary after the fashionable extremes of London. Nancy was very young. I, however, could see the distinct possibilities of a match and gave the young people a chance to get to know each other. It didn't take long for them to develop a *tendre* for each other then!"

"I see." Rossmere shifted slightly in his chair, asking casually, "And you consider it a good marriage? They're well-suited?"

"Decidedly. It couldn't possibly be better."

"And do you think," Rossmere hazarded the guess,

"that if Lady Jane and I spend time together, we will decide to marry?"

"I'm sure of it."

Rossmere shook his head. "I can only say that I think it unlikely, on either of our parts. We are, after all, considerably older and more experienced than Mr. Parnham and Lady Nancy."

Mabel scoffed at this suggestion. "Age has nothing to do with it. Adjusting to the advisability of such a match is even simpler than falling in love, my dear Rossmere."

It was an awkward time to bring up the matter of a loan, but Rossmere felt suddenly impatient with her schemes. He wished to settle the matter of his finances without all this extraneous tomfoolery. He was willing to remain at Willow End for the month he'd promised, but not in order to win Mabel's support.

"I've had a letter from my temporary manager," he said. "He's had to make some unexpected purchases for the estate. I wonder if I might impose on you to lend me the necessary sum. Which would include the quarter's mortgage payment as well, of course. I can't depend on receiving payment for the harvest before that's due."

Mabel's lips had set stiffly during his speech. Now she lifted a hand in an apologetic gesture and let it drop back to her lap. "You see what happens, Rossmere? These little emergencies are forever arising. You don't need a temporary solution, you need a permanent one. I don't know that I can see my way clear to lending you sums year after year when you make no effort to restore your fortunes by the only means at hand."

"Marrying a rich woman."

"Marrying my niece, who is a perfectly delightful girl and would bring you a dowry that would solve your difficulties forever."

Rossmere nodded and rose from his chair. "I understand your position, Lady Mabel. You've been very generous and I assure you every shilling of the money you've loaned me will be repaid on our agreed terms. I won't look to you for any further assistance. Now, if you will excuse me."

Mabel looked stricken. "Rossmere," she called after him, "it's for your own good."

"Doubtless," he murmured as he let himself out the door.

7

Jane was disturbed by Rossmere's cool behavior during dinner. Each time she made some effort to engage him in conversation, he offered only a simple answer, giving no indication of any interest whatever in the subject. His bearing was rigid, his mind obviously preoccupied, his face stiffly forbidding.

At first she thought she must have done something to offend him. Then it occurred to her that he had had further speech with her Aunt Mabel on the subject of marriage. Mabel cast little glances in his direction, the way she used to do when she'd punished one of the children when they were young and she wanted to know if she'd yet been forgiven. Either Rossmere did not notice her glances, or he chose to ignore them. The only one he listened to with any sign of tolerance was Lord Barlow, who had started reading the book John Parnham brought him and wished to try out its arguments on his captive audience.

Jane was impatient with the lot of them. Dinner had been a lively affair when the Reedness children were growing up. Each of them would introduce an interesting topic by stating something outrageously provocative. The others would take up cudgels on one side or another of the issue, and soon a heated discussion was raging. Jane sighed. They had been wonderful times.

And then there was Richard to fascinate and challenge her. They had often read out loud to each other, stopping to debate a point or remark on the excitement of the author's ideas. In those days antiquities had been only one of the dozens of subjects that interested her and that she was able to talk about. Now she could discuss menus with Aunt Mabel and Roman and Greek statuary with her father . . . and little else.

When it was time to withdraw for the gentlemen to have their port, Jane said, "I hope you will excuse me. My head is aching and I think I'd best lie down in my room."

"But, of course, my dear," her aunt exclaimed. "I could bring you a damp cloth. How very strange for you to feel unwell."

"Please don't trouble yourself on my account. I'll be quite all right," Jane assured her.

With a brief nod to her father and Rossmere, she hurried from the room and up the stairs to her chamber. She kicked off her white kid shoes and pulled the combs from her hair. Though she had exaggerated about having the headache, her head was racked with disappointments and worries. In her stocking feet she paced restlessly about her sitting room, pausing at the open window to draw a breath of fresh air.

How very dull her life had become! And she'd barely noticed it. Since Richard's death she'd lived a very retired and a very inactive existence. She'd scarcely been on the new mare her father had bought to distract her from the loss of her love. Suddenly she felt she must get outdoors. Inside, with all these stiff and single-minded people, she was close to suffocation.

Since she didn't wish the household to know she was going out, she managed to undress herself, though the sarcenet slip was a chore to release without her maid's help. Getting into her riding habit was scarcely easier. The slate-colored cloth was moderately full and finished up the front with braiding and a ruff at the neck. She pulled on leather boots to match and carried Limeric gloves and a small round hat to cover her loose hair. To avoid running into anyone at the front of the house, she went down the servants' stairs at the rear and slipped out unnoticed.

Her horse had been named Gingerbread by her previous owner. The mare was the color of gingerbread, but Jane imagined the name also referred to Gingerbread's rather spicy disposition. She was a bit ashamed that she'd spent so little time on the obviously eager young horse. When she was handed up into the saddle by the groom, she patted Gingerbread's neck and whispered a promise to do better.

Because they kept country hours at Willow End, it was still early in the evening and still light. Jane guided the mare along her favorite route past the springs and the quarry and the tumuli that had first interested her in antiquities. The footpath she sometimes took to church crossed the trail a little farther on, and she noted that the stile was in need of repair. Beyond the coppice she gave Gingerbread her head and delighted in the smooth strength of the mare's stride.

The tensions that had been accumulating in Jane eased away as she rode. Riding was the one activity where she could clear her mind of the miscellaneous annoyances of her days. How strange that she had recently allowed herself this pleasure so seldom! In future she wouldn't be so stingy.

Gingerbread's endurance was wonderful to behold. She galloped for more than half an hour and showed no signs of fatigue. Finally Jane slowed her to a trot simply because they had come around to the village on the long swing of their ride. The shops in Lockley were closed for the day, but some quirk of curiosity prompted Jane to ride down the High Street instead of taking the trail that skirted the village.

Jane was determined to ride past the Bentwick cottage to see if there was any sign of Mrs. Fulton. If Mrs. Fulton was indeed someone not quite proper to know, would there be a suspicious caller there? Long before Jane reached the cottage, it was quite obvious that there was a caller, and Jane knew precisely who that caller was.

Ascot was tied to the iron ring beside the gate.

A multitude of sensations assaulted Jane. She felt surprise and disappointment, and even some irritation. There were other elements as well, which she could not as easily identify. She was about to urge Gingerbread into a canter when Mrs. Fulton and Lord Rossmere came around the house. The viscount was carrying a basket into which his companion was placing roses that she'd cut with her shears. She was laughing up at him and Jane saw him shake his head with a rueful smile.

Her horse's hoofbeats attracted the couple's attention and they looked up as she rode past. Jane lowered her head in a grave nod before returning her gaze to the road ahead. Mrs. Fulton smiled at her and waved one hand merrily, while Rossmere stared at her looking vexed. Well he might, Jane thought indignantly. The least he could do was to be more circumspect about his dalliance.

She was tempted to kick Gingerbread to a gallop again, but feared Rossmere would think she was trying to hurry away from them. At no point did she look back to see what transpired after she passed, so it was with some surprise that she heard hoofbeats behind her. The closer the horse came, the more skittish Gingerbread became. Jane had her hands full trying to calm the mare and keep her from sidling clear off the road.

When Rossmere drew abreast of her, she snapped, "I told you my mare would dislike being near Ascot. Pray ride on with him."

"She'll settle down in a moment. After all, she's been in the same stable with him for nearly a week."

"It's not the same thing."

"Isn't it?" Something about this struck him as very amusing, for his lips twitched and his eyes sparkled as he watched her try to control the restive horse. "Are you afraid his wildness will infect her?".

"I'm afraid she'll throw me in her agitation," Jane retorted. "I wish you would just ride on."

"Oh, no. Not until you've learned that Ascot is perfectly blameless, as is his rider."

Jane's eyes swept to his face. "Blameless of what?"

"Of anything improper, either of us," he assured her. He reached out and laid a comforting hand on Gingerbread's neck, speaking encouragingly to her in a firm, affectionate voice. The mare's ears flicked back and forth and her erratic tred settled into an ordinary trot. Ascot nudged the mare with his great black muzzle, and she swung her head in a gesture that looked remarkably coy, but she maintained an even pace.

"You see? She's quite used to him now." He sat back in his saddle and considered Jane. "I thought you went to your room with the headache."

"I felt better after a while."

"You were annoyed with me at dinner."

Jane didn't feel civil enough at the moment to deny it. "You were very tiresome. I thought we'd passed the stage where you found it necessary to be cool and distant."

"Your aunt pursued the subject of our marriage again."

Jane shrugged. "What difference does that make? She will discover in time that we mean what we say, that we have no intention of marrying. You needn't be rude to me to prove it."

For a moment he looked as though he meant to say something important. He leaned toward her, the line between his brows becoming pronounced. Then he studied her face and straightened. "I beg your pardon. It won't happen again."

Feeling cheated of his confidence, Jane spoke with an edge to her voice. "You had given me the impression Mrs. Fulton was not an entirely respectable woman. Do you spend a great deal of time in her company?"

"I never said she wasn't respectable."

"Rossmere, let's not bandy words. Your actions indicated that it would be improper for me to strike up an acquaintance with Mrs. Fulton. Is that untrue?"

"No."

"But it's perfectly acceptable for you to renew your acquaintance with her."

"I called on her as a matter of curiosity, Lady Jane. Nothing more." Rossmere's jaw was firmly set. Wisps of his black hair lifted in the breeze. His blue eyes were narrowed with annoyance.

"You think I don't have any right to question your motives, I gather. But I would remind you that as a guest at Willow End your behavior is a reflection on my father. If Mrs. Fulton is a less-than-respectable female, your visits are certain to be construed most unfavorably by the villagers. On the other hand, if her reputation here is all that it should be, your visits could destroy it."

"You're too kind to offer me lessons in propriety, Lady Jane. I'm well aware of the need to honor local custom in the matter. I never even went indoors with her this evening."

Jane sighed. "I'm sure you'll be circumspect, Lord Rossmere."

"What makes you think I could afford to have a dalliance with Mrs. Fulton?"

It hadn't occurred to Jane, until that moment, that anyone would charge Rossmere to dally with her. Surely even mistresses made exceptions for handsome, warm-blooded men? She found the viscount regarding her quizzically and turned her head away.

"You're quite out, you know, if you think such women indulge in acts of charity," he said, amusement lifting his lips.

"I'm sure it's improper for me to think of such women at all."

He laughed. "Probably."

She felt more at ease with him again and they rode in silence until the buildings of Willow End appeared off to the right. "There's a fair at Littleton for the next day or two. I'm to judge the marmalades, jams, jellies, and preserves. I do it every year; they count it a great honor. There are the usual entertainments and stalls. Aunt Mabel won't come along, as she hates fairs. And there's to be racing, which might hold a special interest for you. One of Ascot's colts is running. Would you care to accompany me?"

"One of Ascot's colts? I had no idea Richard had bred him. Is the horse fast?"

"If gossip is to be credited, there's been nothing faster, save his father, in the history of the county."

Rossmere regarded her with a thoughtful frown. "Would you mind if I rode Ascot there, beside the carriage?"

"Not at all."

"Then I can't think of anything I'd prefer doing."

"Excellent. We'll leave directly after breakfast."

The fairgrounds outside Littleton had been used for the August fair for decades. There were tents, booths, and stalls selling toys and trinkets, gingerbread and beer. The weather was perfect, cooler than the last week had been, but sunny, with a light breeze blowing. As usual, there were dwarfs and giants and a magnificent menagerie as well as an educated pig and a man-monkey. Hawkers cried their ballads, showmen readied their Punch and Judy entertainments. Alongside the bookstalls and skittle alleys, pie men and fruit sellers strolled with their wares.

Rossmere left Jane in a booth whose shelves were lined with a multitude of glass jars marked with each maker's name—apple jam, apricot marmalade, black-current jelly, damson jam, gooseberry jelly, greengage jam, quince marmalade. He didn't envy her the necessity of tasting each of them and judging which was best. But he forgot about the booth full of jars the moment he moved with the crowd toward the temporary racetrack.

The Willow End coachman, who had driven Lady Jane, was already there, studying the horseflesh parading in the area. Rossmere leaned against the railing next to Barnes and asked, "Have you a fancy to bet on one of them?"

"Ay, the brown filly. Know the owner, Jeremy Davenport."

"Which one of them is Ascot's colt?"

Barnes pointed to the far end of the enclosure. "The black colt, there by the railing. But he's untried, milord. Don't know that I'd sport my blunt on him. Never in a race before, see. Don't matter that they run like hell if they've never had to run with other horses."

Rossmere studied the colt. Though the horse certainly had the stature of his father, there was no telling if he had the strength and the staying power. "Is it too late to join the field?" he asked.

Barnes' head swung up instantly. "You . . . never! With the wild one? Has he ever raced before?"

"Not that I'm aware of. Is it too late?"

"You can sign up till half hour before post," the coach-man admitted.

A large notice posted beside the track announced that the purse for the race was fifty pounds. But that wasn't the only inducement Rossmere had. He remembered Richard telling him he had always wanted to race Ascot, had in fact given him that name because of his plan. The problem for Richard had been finding someone to ride the unruly horse. Rossmere had no doubt about who would ride Ascot. He wouldn't let anyone else do so on a bet.

The entry fee was five shillings. The viscount paid his money to a man who noted his tonnish dress with some apprehension. The fellow scratched his grizzled head energetically, saying, " 'Tis a hard ride, sir. The young 'uns don't pay much mind to keeping the order."

"You needn't fear for me," Rossmere assured him. "My horse will keep a way clear for himself."

As he walked away, he decided not to bring Ascot to the enclosure until just before the race. It was true enough that he would fidget among the other horses, perhaps even rebel at being forced to wait with them at the starting line. Rossmere considered his strategy as he drifted around the fairground, buying gingerbread and brandy balls, a sausage on a stick and a peach and an ice. He watched three jugglers and bought an old book about Bath for Jane with the last three shillings he had on him.

Now he really would have to win the race, he thought grimly. There was very little left in his drawer at Willow End.

He decided that he wouldn't tell her about the race. Not only would she likely disapprove, but he understood that the judging would take the better part of her day. He passed the booth with its rows of jars on his way to get Ascot. Jane stood with two other women, distinguished by her elegant height. Rossmere paused to watch her, unobserved, as she chatted with her fellow judges. He was struck by this view of her: she was teasing about something, her eyes dancing with merriment. He had thought her rather stiff and dowdy when he arrived at Willow End a week ago. How was it that he now thought her not only genuinely warm, but devilishly attractive as well?

With an impatient shrug he took himself off to the stable where he'd left Ascot. There was sufficient time before the race to walk Ascot in the enclosure with the other horses, but Rossmere wasn't sure it was a wise idea. Better, perhaps, to keep his half-wild animal as far away as possible until the last minute.

His decision to lead Ascot around the long way to the racetrack only avoided the crowd for a short while. As they encountered more and more people hurrying past, Ascot began to prance with nervousness. Holding him firmly by the bridle, Rossmere walked him quickly past the swinging rides set up for children. Ascot snorted and tossed his head, his eyes rolling wildly at the unfamiliar activity. When a pebble from a slingshot stung his hind-quarters, he very nearly knocked the viscount over with his bucking.

Matters were not proceeding well, Rossmere decided when he had managed to bring Ascot into the enclosure. The other horses made him even more jittery. Rossmere swung up into the saddle and rode his horse away from the most heavily congested area. But there were horses all around the enclosure, and Ascot continued to exhibit his displeasure. Rossmere found it uphill work keeping his mount from exhausting himself with plunging away from the other animals.

It was clear that Ascot wasn't going to line up easily with the other animals. There were almost a dozen horses in the race, and most of their riders were whooping and shouting with excitement. Ascot's ears were flat back against his head now and he lunged when Rossmere directed him toward the starting line, again and again.

A less-persistent man might have abandoned the job at that point. Rossmere motioned a lad over to him and said, "Tell them I'll hold him about twenty feet back from the others, but that we're still in the field."

"That's no way to run a race," the boy insisted, disgusted. He spat into the dirt and added, "You won't never be able to catch up with them."

"Don't bet on it," Rossmere said just as he caught sight of not one but two familiar faces in the crowd that lined the railings. He might have known that Lady Jane's coachman would pass along word of his entry to her. But he hadn't expected to see Madeline Fulton, in a dashing red carriage dress with a red parasol, standing just a few feet away from her.

8

Barnes had sent a message with Tilly, Jane's maid. At first Jane had thought the girl must be mistaken, until she excused herself from the judging for a while to check out the story. Standing by the railing, watching him try to control the wild horse, she had felt a tremor of fear. What could have possessed Rossmere to enter a horse race at a country fair? Both he and the horse were inexperienced and would very likely do an injury to themselves. Even if he was able to forget, she never did. Richard had died from a fall off Ascot.

She had only mentioned the race because of Ascot's colt being in it. Her thought had been that Rossmere would enjoy seeing the colt run, not that he would decide to enter the race himself.

The local people were amused by Rossmere's attempts to bring Ascot in line. The resentment they might have felt that a viscount who was merely visiting in the area had decided to join the race was not evident. They made laughing remarks about his horse and his capabilities, assuming that the position he was forced to take would necessarily mean he would finish the race dead last.

Jane doubted it. She had seen Ascot run. Unfortunately, or fortunately, depending on how one looked at it, the other horses disturbed him. His naturally reckless temperament was obvious to everyone. People had begun to whisper that it was Richard's horse. She heard Richard's name on the wind, bandied about in an almost superstitious way, with people ducking their heads as they spoke it.

Eyes turned her way. She stood a little taller, a little prouder, her hands folded together behind her back. Let them stare at her. They often had when Richard was alive, thinking her extremely odd to have attached herself to a madman. Perhaps, when she was very young, it had bothered her to be so unkindly judged by all and sundry. With age had come a calmness, a composure that was more of a rebellion than any of them suspected, because it was a rejection of their values rather than an ignorance of them.

But she was furious with Rossmere. Not because he had put her in this position of being discussed again by her inquisitive neighbors. Rather because she questioned his motives in entering the race. Jane had seen Mrs. Fulton nearby and had noticed the widow waving gaily to Rossmere.

Reason tugged uselessly at her mind. Everyone was there urging someone on, and Rossmere was the only one Mrs. Fulton knew. Yes, and she was clapping her hands with delight and calling out his name. How had she even known he would be here today? Jane hated to consider the possibility that he had returned to her cottage sometime during the night. Better to imagine that he had run into her at the fair and disclosed his plan. It would certainly be an incentive for her to cheer him on.

Just at that moment Rossmere caught her eye. He tipped his head to her, a wide grin spread on his face. Oh, definitely, the gesture was for her. As close as Mrs. Fulton was, it could not have been meant for anyone else. Even Jane's nearest companion, one of the other jam judges, remarked on it in her own particular fashion.

"Did you see that? How very forward of the fellow, I must say. Do you know him, Lady Jane?"

"Yes, indeed! It's Lord Rossmere, who is staying with us at Willow End. I believe this is his idea of a joke."

"My, my! Imagine. How very odd in him, to be sure. And isn't that the horse Richard Bower owned?"

"It's Ascot. One of his colts is running in the race. I'm sure that's what put the idea in Lord Rossmere's head. The black colt, on the end there."

"A proper beauty," Miss Caruthers admitted. "Much better behaved than his lordship's horse."

The crack of the starting pistol interrupted any further attempt at conversation. Jane couldn't tell how she felt any longer. The anger, the fright, the amusement, all seemed to roil inside her until all she wanted to do was be back in her room at home, reading a nice, undemanding book. But her eyes were glued to the race. Almost immediately the mass of horses surged forward, jockeying for position. Far behind the main bunch was Ascot.

Rossmere rode as he did every day when he gave Ascot his head, hunched slightly forward with heels at the ready. He didn't play his whip as the other riders did. By voice and hands alone he appeared to urge his horse to lengthen his stride. As they gained ground on the field, the viscount kept Ascot well to the outside of the other horses, an obvious attempt to avoid any untoward incidents. It was a boisterous field, however, and the riders who had already determined that they had no chance of winning were not averse to disrupting the proceedings.

When Ascot came up on the outside of the field, the last horse drifted over into his path, his rider waving his whip wildly in the air and yelling heartily. Rossmere simply let Ascot intimidate both horse and rider by thundering right up on them. Jane watched as the horse was jerked back to the side, presenting no problem for the passing Ascot. She realized, though, that Rossmere had started from a great disadvantage and it seemed next to impossible that Ascot would be so much faster than the others that he could overcome this handicap.

The course of the race was mainly within sight of the spectators, because the crowd stood on a slight rise. The horses passed over a wide stretch of turf, through a small wood, over a rise where they were lost from view for only a few minutes before the leading horses were jumping a stream and winding around a fenced field and along a thorny hedgerow. Jane watched with mounting excitement as Ascot surged forward, jumping the stream with ease.

The huge black beast passed horse after horse. Jane could feel her heart pounding painfully in her chest. Her clammy hands were bunched at her sides, and her lips tightly pressed together so she wouldn't call out anything unsuitable. One swift glance assured her that Mrs. Fulton was just as much involved in the spectacle before them, and a lot less restrained.

When there were only two horses still in front of him, and one directly beside him, Ascot seemed to stumble. To Jane's astonishment, Rossmere grabbed the whip from the rider beside him and tossed it away into some gorse bushes.

"Did you see that?" a man at her elbow exclaimed. "Ned Sommers tried to trip that other horse with his whip. I'll be damned. And that black-haired fella just flips his whip out of the way. There's a downy one for you."

Ned Sommers and his horse quickly fell back as Ascot once again pounded onward. A brown filly and the black colt were running almost neck and neck. There was only a matter of a dozen or so yards left to the finish line. Rossmere used his whip now, once, to spur Ascot to an even more determined effort. Jane was astonished to see that there was still strength left in the magnificent animal. Ascot drew abreast of the other two horses.

The finish line loomed before them. Jane noticed that an astonished hush had fallen over the crowd. In the relative silence she heard Rossmere's voice calling "Now!" and watched as Ascot pulled ahead the few necessary inches to win the race. She never knew which of the horses came in second. It didn't seem to matter.

A shiver ran down her spine as a great cry went up, until she realized that it was a spontaneous expression of admiration rather than disappointment that one of the local favorites hadn't won the race. Jane saw Mrs. Fulton dancing about in a most undignified way—and wished that she were able to do precisely the same thing.

"Well, that was tremendously exciting," Jane's companion said, "but we'd best get back to the jam judging or we'll never finish."

Jane wanted to stay where she was and see what happened next, but she allowed Miss Caruthers to lead her off. All sorts of uncomfortable sensations continued to rage in her, not the least of which was a decided jealousy that Mrs. Fulton was going to be there to greet Rossmere and she wasn't. Well, not jealousy, perhaps, but certainly envy, Jane amended mentally. In order for her to be jealous, she would have to have some special interest in Rossmere. Which she did not.

When the exhausting job of judging was finished and they had awarded the ribbons for prizes, Jane found Rossmere standing outside the booth waiting for her. His head was cocked to one side, as though he expected some remark from her on his performance. Jane felt tongue-tied. Nothing she could think of to say was appropriate: not scolding him for entering the race with Ascot, or keeping one of the local people from winning the money, or even praising him for winning, since it seemed disloyal to Richard, somehow. She had realized as she watched the viscount ride that he handled the horse even better than Richard had.

"You've had an exciting day," she finally murmured. "Willow End will seem a little flat after this, I fear."

His brows lifted. "Is that all you have to say about the race, Lady Jane? I expected a great deal more from you. Don't tell me you have subjects that you won't discuss," he teased.

"Very few," she assured him. "You rode very well and Ascot was quite remarkable. Will that do?"

"It will have to, won't it?" He guided her through the crowds toward her carriage. "Did you know that he'd sired both the horses he triumphed over in the end?"

Jane regarded him sharply. "So I heard. They're both rather better-behaved than Ascot."

"You can't expect a prime goer to be tame, my dear. Ascot has more heart than the average. He's extraordinarily spirited, in fact." He stopped suddenly, drawing her to a standstill beside him. "This has something to do with Richard, doesn't it? Do you think I dishonored his memory by riding his horse in a country race? If you do, you're right out, you know. He had always intended to race Ascot, if he could find the proper rider."

It didn't matter that she hadn't known that. Of course Richard had had dreams she knew nothing about. That was always the case, no matter how close two people were. But she could feel a stinging at her eyes. Ridiculous! Where was her lauded self-control, her remarkable calm? And why did Rossmere have this wretched effect on her?

"I wish you will let go of my arm," she said stiffly.

His fingers instantly released their urgent grip. "I do beg your pardon, Lady Jane. I meant no disrespect."

"Of course not," she agreed with a forced smile, intent on relieving the charged situation. His dark eyes remained fast on her face. There was something in them that made her breath halt momentarily, her hands twist at her sides. "I've had an exhausting day," she forced herself to say casually. "Barnes will be waiting to drive me home."

"He is. That's where I'm taking you."

Jane absently brushed down her skirts and followed him past the stalls wafting aromas of sweets and savories. Her stomach rebelled after the constant tasting of jams, but she would have loved a cup of tea and a piece of bread and butter. It seemed too difficult to pluck at his sleeve now and ask him to stop, so she hurried after his solid, splendid figure as he cleared a path for her.

When they reached the carriage, she found that a pot of hot tea and a plate of warm bread spread with butter was laid out for her. She blinked in surprise. There was a book, too, laid out on the seat. Her hand instinctively went out to it.

"I thought you might wish a quick refreshment before we headed back," Rossmere explained, his voice roughened by irritation. "If you shouldn't like it, we can quickly clear it away."

"How very thoughtful of you! I can't think of anything I'd like more at the moment." She glanced at the book and raised her brows in query. "Where did this come from, my lord?"

"It's a book I found at the fair and thought you might enjoy. You've mentioned Bath a number of times. Perhaps you already have it."

"No, not this one. Thank you so much." She seated herself on the comfortable squabs and patted the spot beside her. "Come and join me, Lord Rossmere."

"Thank you, but only for a moment. If I don't claim Ascot from the urchin I've allowed to hold him, I may never see the horse again." He accepted a cup of tea and asked her about the judging of jams and jellies.

"It very nearly kills my taste for such things from one year's fair to the next," she admitted. "There was nothing much out of the ordinary today, though Mrs. Hotchkiss's apricot jam was particularly good and we found mold in one of the raspberry jellies."

"And you do this every year?"

Jane hastily covered a yawn so extravagant that it threatened to dislocate her jaw. How tired she was! The tea would undoubtedly revive her; in the meantime she forced her tired eyes wider open. "Every year, yes. It's expected of me. Oh, and did I tell you the tenants at Graywood have given me notice that they're leaving? If I'd known just a little sooner, I'd have made a point of seeing several people at the fair. There are always certain families who seem to know who's looking for a place, at any given time. But never mind. I can take care of that later."

Rossmere studied the forced brightness of her face and set down his empty cup. "I'd best rescue Ascot. I'll see you back at Willow End."

Jane nodded and watched him move away. "Thank you so much for the book," she called. "It was very kind of you."

Since she didn't see Rossmere on the road, Jane felt certain he had preceded them the whole way. As her carriage swung up the drive to Willow End, Jane was surprised to see John Parnham just climbing out of his landau in front of the entry stairs. There was no sign of Nancy, and certainly neither of them was expected. A current of alarm ran through her. She could barely wait for her own carriage to draw to a stop before pushing open the door and jumping to the ground.

Parnham had waited on the stairs for her, a worried look on his face. "You've been out, then," he said, "and won't know if Nancy really did come here."

"I wasn't expecting her," Jane replied. "I've been at the fair all day."

"Ah, yes, the Littleton fair. Nancy had mentioned how much she enjoyed it as a child. Perhaps that's why . . ."

"Why what?"

He appeared slightly embarrassed. "Why she insisted on coming here today. I was out, and when I returned to the hall, they told me she'd taken the old carriage and headed for Willow End. I couldn't imagine why."

Jane had the sinking feeling that she was being drawn into one of the distortions Parnham had recounted on his previous visit. Without bothering to reply to his last comment, she hastened up the stairs and through the door Winters already held open. "Is Lady Nancy here?" she asked.

"Yes, my lady. In your sitting room." The old man wore a puzzled frown. "She seemed to be under some misapprehension as to your health."

"My health?"

"She thought you were suffering from a severe indisposition."

There was a grunt from behind her, as if Parnham had heard this and was trying to stifle his disbelief. She refused to honor his act with any attention. "I shall go straight up to her. Has a room been prepared?"

"The usual one, milady, nearest the nursery."

"Thank you. See that Mr. Parnham is taken care of, won't you?" She started up the stairs, but turned to ask, "Has Lord Rossmere returned?"

"Not as yet."

Where the devil could he have gotten himself to? she wondered. There wasn't time to give any thought to the matter, though, as she was most concerned about her sister. She found Nancy seated at the window, staring out over the lawns shadowed in the late-afternoon sunlight. Nancy raised her eyes to Jane's face, a wary look tightening her usually soft face.

Jane sat down opposite her sister and grasped her hands. "John has arrived and says you came here without his knowledge. I'm not swayed by what he says. Just tell me how you think it was, what you know has happened."

Nancy shivered. "I was in the garden, cutting flowers. John came out to me, hurrying as if something were the matter. I thought immediately of William. But he said there had been a messenger from Willow End, that you were very ill and wished me to come to you. John said that I should go ahead, with William, and that he would follow when his more-pressing appointments were taken care of. When I got here, I found that you were not only not ill, but not here at all. I've been sitting here all afternoon. I don't know what to do, Jane." Her voice trembled. "This isn't the first time this sort of thing has happened."

"In what way do you mean that? Do you feel there is something the matter with you, or that John is . . . playing some kind of trick?"

"I'm not aware of anything being wrong with me, but . . ." Nancy stopped and turned her hands over in a helpless gesture. "What possible reason could there be for him to play a trick? He's so certain that he's right, I begin to doubt my own senses."

"Don't do that, I beg you!" Jane pressed her sister's cold hands. "Let me tell you what he told Father the last time you were here."

She related the incidents Parnham had enumerated, watching Nancy's face carefully for signs of disturbance. Long before she had finished, Nancy was simply shaking her head and muttering, "No, no."

"Did those things not happen?" Jane asked when she had finished.

"Only two of them. You remember my laughing about thinking William's hands were on backward. And there was an invitation from our neighbors. I swear it, Jane. I saw it with my own eyes. But then, it seems there wasn't."

"I'm sure there was," Jane said with firm conviction. "Don't let yourself doubt it, my love. There's something happening here that we can't understand, and I think it would be wise not to make matters worse by insisting that your husband is wrong. Will you trust me in this?"

Nancy drew a long, shaking breath. "Absolutely. I know you want only what's best for me. You always have."

"We'll go downstairs and speak with John. I think it would be a mistake to avoid him. You will say only that there was a misunderstanding. Don't accuse him of anything. Don't be pushed into an admission that you were wrong. Meet every objection with a smile and your acceptance that there has been a misunderstanding. Can you do that?"

"I think so." Nancy held her sister's hand against her flushed cheek. "You do believe me, don't you?"

"Yes, I believe you."

Rossmere had returned with very little time left to change for dinner. It was not until he joined Lady Mabel, Lord Barlow, and Lady Jane in the gold drawing room that he realized there was additional company. There was also a very strained atmosphere in the room. The lines on Lord Barlow's face seemed more deeply etched than usual, and Rossmere's godmother was fluttering about in a rather aimless way, attempting to smooth matters out.

Though he tried to catch her eye for some enlightenment, Lady Jane refused to even glance at him. She stayed glued to her sister's side, smiling encouragement to the poor child. Rossmere had not seen Nancy look so pale and drawn before. Her husband was wonderfully solicitous.

"A misunderstanding. Yes, yes," Parnham declared. It was plain to all that he was bravely brushing aside his great concern, making light of the matter. "And here is Lady Jane in the peak of health, to be sure. How good of you to make room for us at your table on a moment's notice, Lord Barlow. I understand my dear sister has been at the fair all day. I think perhaps the fair has a great appeal to Nancy as well. We will be sure to take it in tomorrow on our return to the hall."

Rossmere watched Nancy's face during this recital. The young woman said nothing, but her eyes grew large and almost fearful. He saw Lady Jane squeeze her hand and continue to hold it tightly. When he had had quite enough of Parnham's display, he interrupted the steady flow to say, "Have you heard that Ascot won the race at the fair today?"

Very gratifying to have everyone's attention, of course. Nancy relaxed during his recital of the race, and Parnham smiled but tapped a foot with impatience. Lady Mabel frowned and Lord Barlow chuckled at the story. But it was Jane's reaction that interested Rossmere. And that he couldn't see, for she had turned her head aside and continued in that posture until they all went in to dinner.

9

Jane could tell it was very late at night. There wasn't even a trace of gray beyond the thin summer draperies. The stillness was unbroken by household or outdoor sounds. And yet something had awakened her. Some sound or some movement. As her eyes grew accustomed to the darkness, she scanned her bedchamber for an intruder, but she could see no one.

Her heart beat a little faster than normal. Whether this was fear or simply the effect of an abrupt awakening, she couldn't be sure. Jane was not accustomed to feeling fear in her own home. She sat up in bed and drew the bedclothing around her, though the night was warm. Sitting very still, she waited for some indication of what was amiss.

Everything was silent for several minutes. And then Jane felt sure she heard a noise farther off in the east wing, where Rossmere and the Parnhams had their rooms. The sound was not repeated, though Jane listened intently for some time. Considering the circumstances of Nancy's arrival, Jane decided she should investigate. It might be the nursemaid trying to find Nancy's room in the dark, or it might be something else.

The floor was cold under Jane's feet as she padded quickly across the room. Silly as it was, she hesitated in opening her wardrobe door. No one was hiding there, waiting to pounce on her. What a vivid imagination she had suddenly developed! This was not the kind of thing she'd meant when she had bragged of her imagination just the other day to Lord Rossmere.

What would it mean if he was the one abroad in the house at night? Jane didn't for a moment suspect him of planning to abscond with the silver to repair his fortunes. For one thing, it would be far too obvious who had done it. But there was Mrs. Fulton in Lockley . . . What if he had slipped out of the house and gone to visit her? It was a possibility she couldn't entirely dismiss from her mind.

She slid her arms into the cotton robe and drew the sash tightly about her waist. Though she walked determinedly toward the door, she opened it with a good deal of caution. After all, she didn't wish to alarm anyone who might be out there on some legitimate purpose. In a well-run household, the doors do not squeak, and Willow End was a well-run household. She opened the door silently and stepped out into the black hall.

Ordinarily the wall sconces remained lit during the night, though it wasn't unknown for the candles to burn down and extinguish themselves. Jane had given specific instructions to avoid this situation, however, with visitors in the house. Nancy's nursemaid might have to find her, or the viscount need to make his way to the dining room for a late-night glass of port. For those unfamiliar with the house, the candlelight was a necessary aid. The fact that there was none might explain whatever noises Jane had heard.

And then again, it might be the other way around. As she slowly made her way to the bend in the corridor, she noticed that there was no light coming from beyond, either. She reached up to the sconce as she passed and felt for the candle. Plenty of it left, and no special breeze here to blow it out. When she turned the corner, she could see that the entire stretch of hallway was black, which meant another two sconces had been tampered with. Obviously some mischief was afoot. She stood still and listened for any sound in the night.

Along this hall, the outer edge of the east wing, were the best guest rooms. Nancy and Parnham had the room closest to the stairs going to the third floor, where the nursery was located and where the nursemaid shared a room with little William. At the farthest end of the hall was Rossmere's room, some distance away from the stairs and any possible noise from the nursery. The hall was empty, no light shone under any door, and the door to the third floor was closed. Jane stood for some time trying to decide what to do next.

"What are you doing up, Lady Jane?" a quiet voice demanded.

Jane nearly jumped out of her skin. Rossmere stood directly behind her and she hadn't heard a sound. Where had he come from? Surely if he'd followed her along the corridor, she would have noticed some groaning floorboard or the shush of his feet. She noticed that he wore a nightshirt and his feet were bare.

"I might ask you the same," she whispered back. For some reason it seemed unwise to speak in a normal voice. "I heard a noise. Or I thought I did. Was it you who put out the sconces?"

"Why would I do that? I'm not accustomed to going about the halls in the middle of the night like a phantom footman snuffing the candles."

"Then why are they out? Someone has done it."

"I'm sure I don't know how it happened. Perhaps someone opened a combination of doors and windows that created a severe draft. I wouldn't let it bother me if I were you."

"Wouldn't you?" Jane rolled her eyes with disbelief.

"If it's such an unimportant matter, what are you doing wandering around the halls?"

"Like you, I thought I heard a noise, but I haven't found anything. I'll walk you to your room."

"That won't be necessary."

"My dear ma'am, it would be positively uncivil of me to leave you here alone," he assured her, a touch of amusement tugging at his lips. "Just think of the dangers lurking in the corridors. Candle-eating monsters at the very least. To say nothing of thumping, rambunctious ghosts cavorting in the darkness. It would be most unchivalrous of me to leave you to your own resources at such a time."

"You mock me, Lord Rossmere." But she allowed him to clasp her elbow and turn her in the direction of her chamber. There was something compelling about his presence, an underlying current that she couldn't quite put her finger on. It might have been that he was trying to cajole her out of any fears she might have. Or it might have been that he was largely undressed.

One didn't see a man in his nightshirt every day. It reached to just below his knees. Jane felt rather drawn to him in this unruly state. His hair was disordered by sleep and his chin bristled with beard growth. But his eyes were alert and the hand on her elbow felt warmly protective. Not that Jane needed his protection. She was perfectly capable of fending for herself in her own home. It was just that . . . Well, never mind, she told herself.

Rossmere stopped in front of her sitting-room door. Jane realized that he had no way of knowing it was not her bedchamber. If he had seen her enter at any time, it was certainly by this door. She thanked him now and slipped inside. A form rose up in front of her and she let out a startled yelp. When she realized it was Nancy, with her finger to her lips in a gesture begging for quiet, she stifled the sound. Too late, of course. Rossmere had undoubtedly heard it. Instantly she moved to block the door, which was already opening behind her.

"Are you all right?" he demanded. "What is it?"

"I'm sorry. I've just stumbled over my . . . my books in the dark. At first I thought it was an animal. A candle-eating monster," she forced herself to say with a laugh.

"I'll come in and look around."

"Oh, no! Thank you, but I'm perfectly safe in my own room, Lord Rossmere." She clasped the door handle with one hand and the frame with the other, effectively barring his entry.

Rossmere studied her with suspicious eyes for a long moment. "Very well. If there's a problem, just come out in the corridor and yell. I'm a light sleeper."

"Certainly. Thank you. Good night." She shut the door after him with a decided thump. Then she positioned herself against it, waiting to hear his footsteps in the hall. There wasn't a sound. "If you don't leave immediately," she muttered against the heavy panel, "I will think you have some idea of molesting me."

A muffled expletive, followed by softly stomping feet, issued from the other side of the door. She grinned at her sister, but Nancy looked so terrible that the smile instantly disappeared. "What is it?" Jane asked in the softest of whispers. "No, wait. Don't say a word until we're in my bedchamber."

Jane led her trembling sister through the connecting door and over to the enormous bed. Though Nancy already wore a robe, Jane put her own around the younger woman's shoulders and drew the bedclothes up when she sat down against the pillows. "You've had a fright, haven't you? Shall I bring you a glass of brandy?"

Nancy clutched at Jane's nightdress. "Please don't leave me. I don't need anything as much as your company."

"Very well." Jane climbed into the bed and sat holding her sister until Nancy grew calmer. The trembling became occasional shudders, and some color finally reappeared in Nancy's face. Jane waited for her sister to speak, knowing it would be unwise to start asking question before she was ready.

After what seemed a very long time, Nancy drew a shaky breath and said, "I shall tell you just what happened and you may decide for yourself what it means. I'm sure it won't be the story John tells. I was sound asleep . . ." She paused for a moment, trying to control the wobbling of her voice. "I'm sure it wasn't William's cries that woke me. It was John shaking my arm, telling me that William was crying."

"And could you hear him once you were awake?"

"No. He and the nursemaid, Sarah, are on the floor above, and not directly over our room. I suppose in the dead of night one might hear his cries if he was indeed very loud, and he can be. But I couldn't hear a thing when I tried, and John seemed to be making a lot of noise rustling about in the bed and talking and wondering if Rossmere could hear him and saying he would go up to take care of the matter."

"Is that something John does?" Jane asked, surprised.

"Oh, no. It is merely his way of making me feel bad so that I will do whatever it is." She sighed. "You have no idea how intricate marriage is, Jane. It's more complicated to negotiate than a quadrille."

"Perhaps it's just John, my dear."

"No, I think it's this way, more or less, with most married couples. I'm quite serious. I once mentioned it to Margaret and she just smiled and said these were the adaptations men and women made when they married."

"Gracious. You are certainly strengthening my resolve not to marry, Nancy. But go on."

"Yes. Well, John muddled around for a bit while I assured him that I would go. I still couldn't hear a sound from the floor above, but I wasn't sure I'd be able to with all the fuss he was making. He sulked a bit, as though he were doing me a favor by letting me be the one to take care of the matter."

Jane refused to comment on this.

"So I left him climbing back into bed as I shut the door. The candle was lit in the sconce beside the door to the third-floor stairs. I expected that, because you remember that sort of thing. When I'd glanced around our room, I hadn't seen the candle I came to bed with, but I had decided I wouldn't need it just to reach the baby's room. Those stairs are very steep, as you know, but there was a light at the top as well."

"Did you hear the baby crying by the time you were on the stairs?"

"No. It was completely silent. But I knew better than to go back to John without at least setting eyes on the sleeping baby, so I climbed the stairs and opened the nursery door very quietly. I had to stand there for a minute to let my eyes adjust to the darkness in the room. The sconce in the hall isn't located so that much of the candlelight penetrates into the room, and the baby's crib was all the way on the other side. John had made a great fuss about wanting it near a window where there would be a breeze if the night was hot. He doesn't seem to concern himself with these things at home."

Nancy was silent a moment, and Jane noticed that she shuddered again before drawing a deep breath. "I walked across the floor after a while and stood by the crib. William's breathing was deep and regular, the way it is when he's fast asleep. Sarah's bed was close by, and she, too, was sleeping peacefully. I don't know why finding them asleep upset me, but it did. Or perhaps it was then that the little light penetrating the room disappeared."

"I'm sorry. I don't understand what you mean."

"The room became blacker. It didn't occur to me at first that it was because the candle in the hall had gone out, but I realized that was the case after a moment. Perhaps the draft from opening the nursery door had extinguished it. In any case, when I came back out into the hall, there was no light at all."

"Strange." Jane felt a bristling at the back of her neck. Like a dog whose hackles have risen, she thought. "What did you do then?"

"There really wasn't much I could do. Perhaps I should have hunted around for Sarah's candle, but I would have been fumbling in the dark. And I was raised in this house. I know the stairs down from the third floor. I'd shut the door at the bottom, or it had blown shut. There was no light from the bottom now, either, and the stairwell was even blacker than the upstairs hall."

Nancy shuddered and hugged herself. "I had an awful feeling about it, but I told myself not to be such a pea goose. After all, what could possibly be wrong? So the candle was out; it didn't mean there was anything to be afraid of. I hesitated at the top of the stairs, then started down. There's no handrail, so I put my hands on the wall on either side. The steps are much deeper than you expect. You put a foot down and it seems to meet the tred too late and with a thump. Do you know what I mean?"

"I think so." Jane's skin had begun to crawl. "Go on."

Nancy moistened her lips. "I'd taken two steps down, enough to begin to judge the distance and stop feeling shaky about it. In a second I would have charged on down the rest of the steps, just to prove I wasn't afraid. But I thought I heard something. Not from the nursery floor, but from down below. As I started to step forward, I paused, just for a second.

"I was in my bare feet, and my toes felt something soft just as I was lifting them to take another step. Oh, Jane, how can I tell you what instant fear gripped me! There shouldn't have been anything on the stairs. I was terrified that I would trip over whatever it was, so I threw my balance backward as quickly as I could. That made me fall onto the step behind me. The riser caught me sharply in the back and knocked the breath out of me. But, you see, I still didn't know what was there in the dark."

Jane pressed her lips firmly together. The suspense had made her throat tighten as though the danger still existed.

"I reached out in the dark and my fingers touched a piece of fabric. I could tell it wasn't an animal, not one of the dogs sitting there. Where my fingers first encountered it, it was soft and loose, but higher . . ." Nancy's voice faded again and a tear slipped down her pale cheek. She cleared her throat and continued. "Higher it was taut, almost like a rope. If I had taken another step, I would have tripped over it and fallen, head first, down those awful, steep stairs."

Her body was shaking again and the tears flowed more freely down her face. Jane hugged her tightly and rubbed her back, trying to comfort and reassure her. "You're all right now. I won't let anything hurt you. Go ahead and cry. There's no shame in being frightened." Jane felt a fury rising in her, destroying her usual calm and eating away at her steady rationalism.

Nancy gulped down the worst of her sobs and used the handkerchief Jane handed her to blow her nose. "I made a certain amount of noise falling back against the stair. I don't know what made me do what I did next. I slid down the stairs on my bottom, thumping the walls from side to side, until I smacked my feet up against the door. The material pulled away from the walls as I carried it with me, and I held it in my hands at the bottom of the stairs. Everything was quiet for a short while and then John opened the door. He didn't say anything."

"You mean he didn't call your name? Didn't ask if you were all right?" Jane questioned, the edge to her voice growing with each word.

Nancy shook her head. "He had a candle and he moved it around, finally bringing it near my face. When he saw that my eyes were open, he nearly dropped it.

That was when he finally asked me if I was all right. I told him that I was fine but that the material—it turned out to be my black shawl—had been stretched across the stairs and I'd almost fallen over it."

"What did he say to that?"

"He told me I must be mistaken. He said that I'd put the shawl around my shoulders before I went upstairs and that it must have fallen off on the steps when I didn't notice it. He said I should be more careful."

"And what did you say?"

"I told him . . ." Nancy put her head down on Jane's shoulder. Her voice came muffled and low. "I said that wasn't what happened, but that I would certainly be more careful in future. I came to stay in your sitting room because I couldn't go back to our room with him. But I wasn't going to waken you."

"Oh, my poor dear. I wish I could think of some possible explanation . . ."

"There is none. And yet I don't understand why he would want to . . . injure me. He didn't say anything except that, as I was all right, he was going back to bed. Why, Jane? What's happening? We haven't had any particular disagreements. How could he do something like that?"

"I don't know. He must be a very evil man. We should tell Papa right away."

"In the morning," she begged. "I'm exhausted. I just want to go to sleep and forget the whole thing for a little while."

"Of course you do." Jane tucked her in and kissed her forehead. "Go to sleep now. You'll feel better."

She stroked her sister's brow until Nancy fell into a heavy slumber. Then she returned to the sitting room, where she was sure she'd seen the black shawl draped over a beige armchair. She struck a flint and lit a candle on the mantel, then held the shawl up to the light. There were two rents in it, about five feet apart. Just the width of the third-floor stairwell.

10

Rossmere was aware of a great deal of coming and going at Willow End the next morning, with the parties involved constantly changing. Most everyone appeared grim-faced and preoccupied. The viscount felt certain this had something to do with the disruption of the previous night, whatever that had been. For hours no one offered him any explanation.

When Lady Jane discovered him on his way to the library after lunch, she frowned and asked, "May I have a word in private with you?"

"If you're quite sure I won't molest you."

"That was merely a ruse to make you go away."

"I know it was. And I'm not at all sure making me go away was a wise thing for you to do."

She glanced sharply at him as they entered the dim room that served as Willow End's library. Shafts of sunlight came through several windows, but the brightness seemed to be absorbed by the hundreds of leather-bound volumes that lined the walls. There was a rich, musty smell to the room that made Rossmere nostalgic for the better days at Longborough Park.

"Do you have any idea what happened last night?" she asked rather cautiously.

He was afraid that if he admitted how little he knew, she would try to keep the matter a secret. And he was very curious to find out exactly what was going on. So he decided to make an ambiguous reply, calculated to force her to press for details. "Only a part of it," he said.

"Well, what part?"

"About the stairs," he said knowledgeably. The noise could have come from no other location.

"You saw Nancy on the stairs?" she asked with patent eagerness.

"No, but I heard her on the stairs." It was obvious, now, that it had been Nancy he'd heard.

Jane was disappointed. "You didn't see Nancy at all?"

"I'm afraid not. But I did notice that all the candles in the sconces were out."

"Yes. That's important, isn't it? There is no reason at all that Nancy should have put out the candles."

"Is someone suggesting that she did?"

Jane stared at her hands for a long moment. Her brows were drawn down and her eyes were clouded with worry. When she raised her gaze to his, she sighed. "I think I will have to trust you, Lord Rossmere. This is too momentous a matter to let it go as it is headed. If there's even the smallest chance that you can help verify what really happened . . ."

There was very little chance that he could, but he made no attempt to halt her confidences. She was truly distressed, and her anxiety infected him with an urgency he couldn't precisely identify. It was all the more alarming because she spoke, even now, in a calm, unemotional voice calculated to strip her speech of any taint of partiality. She was laying before him the facts, as her sister had given them to her. Rossmere withheld any comment until she had disclosed the entirety of the previous evening's events.

"What did your father have to say about all this?" he asked.

Her expression was pained. "He listened very carefully and then with great sadness told us about John's concerns for Nancy's . . . extravagant imaginings since the baby was born."

"I see. So he didn't believe her?"

"No. It's not just that he's taking John's word; Papa feels that Nancy has been different since the baby was born." Jane pushed a strand of hair back with her long, elegant fingers. "Nancy is the baby, and a favorite of all of us. She's rather naïve because of that, perhaps. We managed to keep her away from the harsher elements of life, I suppose. She cries over the plight of chimney sweeps and children in workhouses. She's a very good person."

"And marriage is a bit more real than she expected," Rossmere suggested.

"That's one way to put it."

"I take it Lady Mabel is standing behind Parnham, too, even if it means believing that her niece is imagining things."

"A temporary aberration, she thinks it," Jane admitted with a certain bitterness. "Aunt has a deep and abiding belief that men are much more inclined to honesty and rationality than women. Already she's remembering instances of Nancy's instability as a child. And instances of any number of women she's heard of who have had similar problems after the birth of a child." Jane grimaced. "They're so easily persuaded of her vulnerability. I know her better than that." Suddenly Jane shuddered. "Do you understand what could happen if she returns with him?"

"Yes. But he doesn't strike me as a stupid man. It would be rather suspicious if anything happened to her so soon after this episode. She should be safe for a while."

"But only for a while," Jane cried. "He could blame anything that happened on her shattered nerves. And to have to live with such a devil. I can't bear to think of it."

"Could she live here?"

"I don't think my father would countenance it for very long, feeling as he does. He can be an obstinate man, and the more I press him on this issue, the more firmly he insists that these are delusions of Nancy's." Jane turned her back to Rossmere. "He's gotten it into his head that observing Richard has somehow made Nancy less steady."

"That doesn't seem very likely. On the other hand, you may be too attached to your sister to see the truth of the matter."

Jane swung around to face him. "You don't believe her, do you?"

"I didn't say that. My mind is open to any number of possibilities. However, the kind of instance Parnham has described is a little more than depressed spirits after childbirth, isn't it? Your sister would have to be very disturbed indeed not to remember all the things he says she doesn't remember. But your sister might not be telling the truth either if she's embarrassed by her own occasional odd behavior. You might consider that."

"There's no need for me to consider that, Lord Rossmere. Nancy is telling me the truth. I don't doubt it for a moment."

Rossmere nodded. "I think we have to act on that premise, in any case. If Nancy can't convince your father to let her stay here for the time being, why not have her get 'sick' and need to rest here until she's better."

"I suppose that's what we'll have to do." Jane clasped her hands tightly behind her as she strode around the room. "What's to be done, though, for the long range? She can't go back to him, she can't stay here."

Rossmere stopped her with a hand on her shoulder.

"We'll have to see how things develop, Jane. You mustn't let this overset you."

She shook his hand off and stood glaring at him. "We're talking about my sister's life, Rossmere. Not her happiness or some little whim. That man is trying to kill her, and you tell me not to worry about it."

"He may not be trying to kill her. He may be trying to frighten her, or to drive her crazy."

"Oh, that's *much* better." Her sarcasm bit through the charged atmosphere between them. "Perhaps you haven't taken a long look at the third-floor stairs. Someone falling from the top, pitched forward by tripping over a shawl made into a rope, would almost certainly break her neck. The stairs are extremely steep and there's no railing to grab on to."

Flushed with anger, tense with fear, she still impressed him as a remarkably capable woman. So where did this desire to comfort her, to clasp her against him and protect her, come from? Rossmere supposed it was because she'd had enough trying things happen to her in her life without this added burden. Her flashing hazel eyes, so surprisingly attractive, caught him up in the turmoil of her emotions.

But really, he saw no simple solution to the problem. If Parnham wanted to kill his wife, eventually he would probably succeed. The only real escape Nancy might have was to be bundled off to an asylum, and from everything he'd heard, that fate was worse than death. If Lord Barlow wouldn't protect her, the best possibility he could see was to find out Parnham's motivation.

"I'll need to see the marriage settlement," he said abruptly.

Jane, who had been following an entirely different track, stared at him. "I beg your pardon?"

"If we're going to find out why Parnham is doing this, the first thing I need to know is what's in their marriage settlement. You thought he needed the money she brought, and I'd like to know what the arrangement is in the event of her death."

"The dowry was his outright. Her own property, which is considerably more than the dowry, would go to her children."

"William is safe enough, then," Rossmere declared. "I suppose Parnham would administer any inheritance of his child's, so the money would basically be at his disposal."

"Yes, but I'm sure Nancy would give him any sums he needed now."

Rossmere regarded her with his former coolness. "Perhaps that arrangement doesn't suit him."

"Doesn't suit him," she scoffed. "So he has decided to kill her! Does that seem reasonable to you, Rossmere? Do you think you would be tempted to do away with me in a similar situation?"

"Don't be absurd," he snapped. "That's not what I meant, and you know it."

Her eyes flashed, unrepentant. "I know no such thing. You're quite sympathetic to the notion that a man's pride cannot tolerate his being under a financial obligation to his wife, aren't you? The only difference is that you refuse to undertake the obligation and Parnham has undertaken to rid himself of the source of his annoyance."

"Just a small difference! You must be very distressed indeed to make such a comparison. I can only conclude that your wits have gone begging."

His words lashed out so harshly that she shrank back from him, looking as though she'd been slapped. Her eyes blinked rapidly, and she shuddered, saying, "You're quite right, of course. I don't know what's come over me. That same impotence and frustration that . . . Never mind. It was wrong of me to say such things and I most sincerely ask your pardon."

He stared at her for a long moment before speaking. "You have it. And now, if you will excuse me?"

He knew her stricken eyes followed him as he stalked

from the library, but he couldn't bring himself to offer her comfort. Deep inside he understood that this awful situation had thrown her back into the days of Richard's worst torment, and Rossmere should be sympathetic to her anguish.

How could she even for a moment compare him with Parnham, whom she thought of as evil incarnate? Had she no regard for him at all? Rossmere had thought perhaps Lady Jane was softening toward him, that she had come to view him as a man of some significance in her life. At least as a friend. It was a blow to learn that she despised him.

Jane watched him go, sick at heart. If she had tried, she couldn't have been more insulting to him. His proud stand about marrying for money was a small matter compared with Parnham's wickedness, and yet she had lumped them together as though there were no difference. For some reason she had felt very, very angry with Rossmere.

And why? Because he couldn't completely believe in her sister? Why should he? He hardly knew Nancy, and there was little reason to take Jane's word, since she was obviously biased.

Or was it anger at the viscount for his personal lack of involvement? It couldn't make much difference one way or the other to him if Nancy's life was in danger. In a few weeks he would return to Longborough Park and forget all about their distant problems.

Richard would have believed her. Richard would have found some solution to the dangerous mystery. If he were well, if he weren't locked up for his own safety . . . He wouldn't have stood there staring at her, questioning her every word. What's more, he would have held her, pressed her against his chest, and run his hands soothingly across her back. He would have kissed her eyelids and her forehead and whispered encouraging words in her ear.

Not that she wanted that sort of behavior from Rossmere!

She had forgotten how much more secure one felt when there was a man who loved you, who cared for your concerns and stood by you in your fear. It was unbearable that she should be caught up in this awful situation and Richard wasn't there to stand firm beside her. If she had wanted to call on Rossmere, to have him comfort her, it was simply because he was the only one around who might conceivably be of help. His broad shoulders had seemed more than sufficient to provide some help.

Perhaps he would have, too, if she hadn't offended him. He had gone straight to the heart of the issue when he considered whether little William, too, might be in danger. Jane would have liked having his intelligence and his steadiness on her side.

With a sigh she stepped away from the window. No use thinking about that now. She would go to Nancy and offer what help she could. Certainly her sister must stay at Willow End until something could be done to solve her desperate problem.

Nancy agreed to everything her sister suggested about crying sick and staying at Willow End. And yet, just an hour later Jane found her in the entry hall, wearing her dove-gray carriage dress and carrying a satchel with some of the baby's toys and bread crusts. Her eyes were red-rimmed, but she managed a thin-lipped smile for her sister's encouragement. John Parnham was at her elbow.

"We're off," he said. "I've said my farewells to your father. Never fear that I'll see Nancy gets her rest. It's all a bit trying for her. She should never have insisted on nursing the child herself. There's a wet nurse right in the hamlet beside the hall. We'll contact her the moment we return."

"No," Nancy said firmly. "The doctor said it would do me no harm to nurse William, and it hasn't."

"Whatever you wish," her husband said in a placating

tone that infuriated Jane. "But we really should be leaving."

Nancy offered her cheek for Jane's kiss. With Parnham so close, Jane didn't dare ask her what was happening. It broke her heart to watch the couple walk down the front stair, the nursemaid close behind with William. A terrible dread froze Jane where she stood. Letting Nancy leave this house seemed almost a sentence of death.

Jane moved to the terrace and watched them climb into Parnham's new carriage. As though to highlight the strangeness of their visit, the older carriage waited directly behind it, empty and forlorn. Jane wished she could hide in it and follow them, spirit herself to Parnham Hall to keep a watchful eye on her dear sister.

The coachman set his team in motion, and Jane bit her lip to prevent herself from crying, or crying out. She waved until both carriages were out of sight. Only then did she notice that Rossmere was standing in the drive, his riding clothes dusty from the summer paths, his whip tapping quickly against his boot, a deep frown etching his forehead. Jane felt suddenly overwhelmed by emotion, but she maintained her calm demeanor, with difficulty, and disappeared into the house.

Rossmere went directly to Lord Barlow's study, where he could see the older man through the open door. The earl was staring vacantly out the window, his lips pursed and his hand absently rubbing a small statue that rested in front of him on his desk.

Though he stood there for several minutes, waiting to catch the earl's attention, such a subtle approach proved unsuccessful. Eventually he had to tap quite firmly on the heavy panel of the door to rouse Lord Barlow from his reverie. Even then, the older man stared at him for a long moment, as though he couldn't remember who Rossmere was, before saying, "Ah, yes, Lord Rossmere. Do come in."

Taking the seat indicated, Rossmere rested both hands atop his riding crop and regarded the earl with puzzled intensity. "Did you refuse to let Lady Nancy stay here?" he asked at length.

Barlow frowned at him. "There was no question of her staying here. She wished to leave with her husband and child."

"I find that difficult to comprehend. Whether or not you believe her, she thinks that her husband tried to kill her last night. It's highly unlikely she wished to go home with him."

"What do you know about last night?" the earl demanded.

"I was awakened by some loud noises and went to explore. Unfortunately, the halls were dark and I was too late to encounter Lady Nancy or her husband. Lady Jane told me Nancy's story this morning."

"She shouldn't have."

"Of course she should have. I might have been able to provide some corroboration." Rossmere tapped the crop impatiently. "I'm not at all sure who's telling the truth in this matter, but I can assure you of one thing: if I had a daughter who believed, for whatever reason, that her life was in danger, I certainly wouldn't send her home with her husband without a proper investigation of the circumstances."

"There's nothing to investigate. Nancy has always been a fanciful child, pampered by everyone at Willow End. The strain of motherhood has taken its toll on her."

"Lord Barlow, I don't understand your attitude. Even if you believe every word Parnham has uttered, you must surely see that your daughter is in need of help."

"And her husband will provide it. He's responsible for her now. I have no jurisdiction whatsoever over her since her marriage."

"You have a paternal obligation to her, and it would

be socially acceptable for her to remain here for a while. I don't understand why you wouldn't let her."

"You certainly don't understand," Lord Barlow said coldly. "Nancy didn't ask to stay here. They came to me when their bags had already been packed and announced that they were leaving. I can only assume that it is what she wanted."

Rossmere rose and glared down at him. "It hardly seems likely, does it? Live human beings are so much more bother than statues, aren't they? Well, I hope you won't mind if I spend a little time trying to find out what's going on. For some inexplicable reason, I feel concerned for Lady Nancy."

"We all feel concerned for her, Rossmere. This household has lived with a great deal more mental instability than most. If we're lucky, my daughter's odd behavior will prove temporary. If not . . ." He waved a tired hand. "We took care of Richard until his death. We would do no less for Nancy, if necessary."

Defeated, Rossmere grimaced. There was no convincing Lord Barlow that his daughter might not be ill, that it might be that her husband was an evil man intent on destroying her, one way or another. How easily he'd been convinced, because he had Richard's example so short a time ago. It meant that Rossmere was the only one who found it necessary to do something about the situation.

Rossmere and Jane, of course. But Jane was shackled by every social restriction inflicted on maiden women: she couldn't ride about the countryside asking questions, visit the local dens of (light) iniquity, or confront her brother-in-law with any hope of success. If anything was to be done, Rossmere would have to do it.

He bowed stiffly to Lord Barlow and left the room.

11

It took Rossmere two days to uncover anything of interest. He had discovered a drinking establishment on the Ridgely Road where the occupants were delighted to talk with practiced ease under the influence of drinks bought for them by his lordship, who was a "regular right one," according to these same fellows. They seemed to know everything that was going on in the district, but had submitted nothing more exciting than Parnham's new carriage for his troubles.

On the second night, however, well into the evening, a strapping young man entered the room whom he hadn't seen before. The youth was of a stolid and uncommunicative nature, and it took Rossmere several heavy wets to induce this Jem to remark on whether he'd seen anything out of the ordinary during the last few weeks.

"Can't say as I have," the young man drawled. " 'Cept the horse, mebbe."

"What horse would that be?" Rossmere asked, gearing himself to great patience.

"Reason I thought of it were 'cause of your Ascot, you know. Fine horse, Ascot."

"Yes. He used to be Richard Bower's "

"Know that." The fellow nodded several times thoughtfully. "Saw the race at the fair. Beat out both his filly and his colt. Wouldn't mind havin' a horse like that myself."

"He's half-wild," Rossmere offered. "The stable boys at Willow End hate to have to handle him."

"Stupid boys. Don't know when they have a champion on their hands. Never could abide them high-and-mighty Willow End boys."

"You mentioned another horse you'd seen that was out of the ordinary," Rossmere reminded him.

"Mmmmm." Jem took a long draw on his beer and pursed his lips. "Not out of the ordinary, so to speak. Not the horse, leastways. Just where it was. And whose it was. See?"

"Yes, I see. Where was it?"

Jem motioned with his head toward the town of Lockley. "Standin' in the little wood there. Out of sight, like. But I had business in the woods."

The men around him chuckled and nudged one another in the ribs. Rossmere didn't need to be told that Jem's "business" in the woods was poaching. "This is the little wood behind the Bentwick cottage?"

"Aye. Standing there when I went in, standing there when I went out."

"How long were you there?"

Jem shrugged his massive shoulders. "Two hour, mebbe. Mebbe longer."

"Whose horse was it?" Rossmere asked as casually as he was able.

"That's the pe-culiar thing, don't you know? It were Clancy's horse."

"And who's Clancy?"

Jem motioned with his head in the other direction. "Farmer down to the hall. Only Clancy were home that night, as it happens."

"How do you know?"

There was more rib-nudging. " 'Cause I went there after. And no horse passed me on the road."

"So do you think Clancy loaned the horse to someone, or was it someone else in his household who borrowed it?"

" 'Tain't no one else there but Maud, and she were there when I come. But Clancy don't loan nuthin', neither."

"But he'd have no objection to hiring it out?"

"Nope. Just the way Clancy likes things, happen. Makes a bob any way he can, does Clancy."

"You don't know who might have hired the horse?" Rossmere pressed.

"No one can afford a horse, needs one. Around here, leastways." Jem leaned back in his chair and pulled again on his beer, satisfied that he had provided as much information as humanly possible.

Rossmere decided it might be best not to press the matter further. If these good people made no connection between the horse and its possible rider, the viscount certainly did. It sounded very like Parnham to rent a horse from one of his tenant farmers if he didn't want to chance recognition of one of his own. Parnham was, after all, the only one who fit all three necessary categories: well-breeched enough to hire a horse, able to afford to hire Madeline, and behaving in such a way as to invite suspicion.

There were, of course, several ways to verify his theory. He could post himself in the wood every night until Parnham came, which might take quite a while, or he could go to Madeline and cajole the information out of her. Time was a matter of importance, however, so he decided his best course was an immediate visit to Madeline Fulton.

As a last gesture of goodwill, he left the landlord with enough coins to cover a round for the entire group, then took himself off as quickly as possible. It was already rather late and he had no idea what kind of hours Madeline kept on nights she wasn't expecting company.

Ascot strained at the bit, eager to stretch his legs over the dark road. He tossed his head and snorted when Rossmere drew him in as they approached the wood behind the Bentwick cottage. It wouldn't do to ride around to the front, where someone from the village might see him enter. As he was sure Parnham did, he guided his horse off the road and wound through the trees. Rossmere scouted the area for any sign of another horse, but found none. After a few minutes of listening to the silent night, he dismounted and walked toward the cottage.

There was a candle burning upstairs in the back room. Rossmere went directly to the rear door and tapped softly on its wooden panel. A warm breeze wafted earthy smells from the kitchen garden and ruffled the viscount's hair. It was only a minute before the door was opened cautiously, and the maid he'd met before craned her head around to inspect him. Her eyes widened when she recognized him.

"Coo, and what do you be wantin', sir?"

"I very much need a word with your mistress. Do you think she would have a moment to grant me?"

"Can't say as how she might. I'd best ask. You wait here and don't go making no noise, hear?"

Rossmere assured her that he would be silent as the grave. He leaned against the door frame while he waited, deciding on what approach would most likely earn him the best information. It wouldn't do to simply ask Madeline outright; she would simply deny any connection with Parnham. He mustn't give any indication at all that he knew what was going on. She was a clever woman and her secrets wouldn't easily be uncovered.

Suddenly she was there before him. Her bright hair cascaded down over her shoulders, and what she wore was elegantly flowing and just barely opaque. Rossmere didn't think it was an article of clothing in which she would receive, say, a neighbor coming to tea. The outline of her breasts was very distinct, and very provocative. She smiled up at Rossmere, mischief tugging the corners of her mouth.

"Now, what would you be doing here at this hour of the night, my lord?" she wondered. "Lost your way, have you? Out riding that magnificent beast of yours and became confused in the dark, I'll warrant. You decided to call at the first cottage that showed a candle."

"Exactly so." He had almost forgotten her skill at weaving fantasies, fantasies that were just right for the person she addressed. And quite different for different men. He recalled someone telling him . . .

"You're in need of succor," she suggested, laying her hand on his arm and gazing up into his eyes. "Some refreshment, some rest, some . . . diversion. And I'm a familiar face, someone who has come to your aid on other occasions. You remember my generosity, my openness, my attention to your needs."

Rossmere did remember their encounters and the ease with which she'd ensnared both his body and his mind. She moved close to him now, until her body was touching his, lightly. And he remembered her body naked, inviting. His gaze shifted from her body to her eyes. There was a sultriness to the green, a sleepy, alluring glaze that suggested she was already aroused. Her hand slid from his forearm up to his shoulder and her head tilted backward, her lips softly pouted for his kiss.

He wasn't going to get any information from her if he rejected this initial advance. So he lowered his head and pressed his lips to hers. How yielding they were! How readily they parted, waiting for his tongue to enter her mouth, to take possession of her. The sensation of her taste, her texture, swept him back to that time years ago when she had been his mistress. He had come to her whenever he chose, and she had given herself to him with such astonishing abandon. He had thought no other woman could possibly be so stimulating.

They were still standing in the rear doorway of the cottage and Rossmere broke off the kiss, saying, "What will your neighbors think?" with a mocking light in his eyes.

"Fortunately my neighbors aren't abroad at this time of night." She tugged at his sleeve, drawing him into the room. "I thought you would come, especially after you won that race at the fair. You were magnificent. But then, you always were magnificent."

It was the kind of flattery that had flamed him to desire in his days with her. Now he concentrated on her reference to the race. He could but assume that she was referring to the prize money. Madeline did not come without price. There were no treats "for the sake of old times." Not with Madeline. What interested him was her apparent willingness to consider a supposed bid from him, when Parnham surely wouldn't like it one bit if he found out about it.

Madeline led him through the kitchen and down the corridor to the front of the cottage. There was a lamp burning in the parlor, where a book lay deserted on the floor and a half-full wineglass rested on an end table. Obviously she had been pleasantly wiling away her evening when he arrived. She motioned to the wine decanter and another glass nearby. "Please help yourself," she said as she lowered herself onto the sofa in a lounging position.

"I don't think you were expecting me," he chided. "Surely this glass was for someone else."

"Merely an efficiency on Mary's part. It saves her the bother of going to fetch another glass if someone calls."

It was possible. Mary struck him as a fairly bright child. Rossmere helped himself to a glass of wine, a very passable Madeira, and approached the sofa where Madeline awaited him, her own glass now in her hands. She patted the spot that would place him in contact with her, since her reclining position occupied the whole of the piece of furniture.

Rossmere looked skeptical. "I wouldn't want to be discovered in an awkward position if a particular friend of yours should arrive." When she started to protest, he waved aside her words. "No, no, you'll never convince me you haven't found some upstart merchant in this area to protect you, my dear. Otherwise you'd never have left London. He must be both wealthy and handsome to entice you to the wilds."

With a little shrug she patted the spot again. "Never mind my current arrangement, Stephen. He won't appear to challenge you to a duel, if that's what concerns you. He never comes this late, and if he should . . . Well, Mary has barred the back door by this time and it would take her an appropriate amount of time to open it, and rouse me, and show him up to my room. Far longer than you would need to disappear out the side window."

In the moderate light of the lamp, he could see that the satin of her gown was a rich gold color. It clung to her hips and lay open somewhat on her legs, just enough to give him a view up to her knees. Rossmere seated himself on a level with her midsection and lifted his glass in a toast. "To a most remarkably beautiful woman." As he sipped, he held her eyes with his, managing, without much difficulty, to look enchanted.

Madeline murmured her pleasure at the compliment, shifting so that one breast swelled above the draped effect of her lounging gown. "And you," she said, raising her glass to him, "are still the most manly devil I've ever laid eyes on."

He shook his head in amusement. "Doing it too brown, Madeline. You've forgotten that pretty phrases pay no toll with me."

"How true! You were always much more interested in other kinds of contact than words. A man of action." She smiled and ran a hand along the satin fabric of her gown from her shoulder to the top of her breast. "You did a lot of talking with your hands, I remember. And they weren't the usual dandy's hands." Reaching across, she picked up one of his hands and traced over it with a slim finger. "Look at that. It's even more rugged than in the old days. Strong, rough, capable, exciting, but unaccustomed to the softness of a female body these days, I'd warrant. I can feel the tautness of it."

"Can you? And is that bad?"

"Only if it's never relieved." Her coquettish smile accompanied a provocative kneading of his fingers. "Why, men's hands have been known to fall off from the continual strain of never being relieved."

"Dear me, what an awful fate. I suppose you could suggest a remedy."

Madeline nodded solemnly. "It's essential that the roughness come in contact with something infinitely soft and remain in contact until there is a total relaxation of the body . . . um, hand. This can't be managed by just touching one spot, though. The hand must be run over a wide area of softness and continually moved about. It has to touch satiny areas, and silky areas, and velvety areas. And it's best if it seeks out warm, moist areas as well. These are all very healing to the hand."

Even her voice was seductive. There was a hoarse edge to the sonorous recitation. Her fingers played coyly with his, her hips pressed forward against his buttocks. Definitely they were moving into dangerous territory. He had thought she would tease him as she had originally, make him wait for full access to her person.

"My hands are more used to reins than to flesh," he admitted. "They would feel rough on your skin. That's not what you're used to."

"I like hands that are firm on the reins, that are firm on my skin. Do you think I'm some kind of pampered doll, Stephen? Have you forgotten that I like to live a stimulating life? That I ride wild horses and enjoy the company of dangerous men? That I take risks other women would blanch at? And you taunt me with your rough hands," she chided him. "I'm not afraid of anything, and I go after what I want. You used to admire that in me. Have you changed your mind?"

"Penury is daunting, my dear. It's easier to live an exciting life if one doesn't have to worry about where one's next meal is coming from."

Madeline regarded him with shrewd eyes. "Hardly one's next meal in your case, Rossmere. But it's true that the prospect of a future lack of funds is unsettling. You should find yourself a wife with a fortune."

"So my godmother tells me. I might offer the same advice to you with regard to a husband. You're no more likely to take it than I am," he insisted, and watched the flicker in her eyes.

Her immediate intention of denying it was quickly overcome by prudence. She lowered her eyes. "There's no future for me in marriage," she said. "Men are so insistent on the exclusive use of their wives. I can't tell you how dull that sounds to me." She laughed, but it had the false ring of being forced. "I can't imagine any man I'd wish to be leg-shackled to."

"No? Well, it's the same with me, Madeline. I'd rather starve than be tied to a woman and her fortune. My very nature rebels against it."

She placed his hand on the satin above her breast. "You would find ways to circumvent the ties, my dear Rossmere. Men always do."

Because she expected it of him, he allowed his hand to cup her breast and slid his fingers over the cool satin where the bump of her nipple invited his touch. He kept his thoughts firmly on what he believed to be her motivations. Probably the very prospect of marriage, despite her recognition that it was the wisest course for a woman of her age and reputation, drove her to recklessness and an attempt to get away with as much as she could. Which explained her willingness to dally with him.

Did she understand that Parnham was actually planning to murder his wife?

Madeline shifted so that the satin robe was pulled back from over her breast. Rossmere's bare hand touched her silky skin. It had been a very, very long time since he'd had this kind of contact with a woman. He was deluged with desire and the memory of heady satisfaction this particular woman had provided in the past. He needed to keep his mind clear, though, and use this occasion to learn what he could. His physical needs were of lesser importance, though they raged through him now with the force of a summer storm.

He continued to fondle Madeline's breasts. With her cooperation he even brushed back the satin from her other breast and cupped it firmly. He rubbed the nipple between thumb and forefinger, feeling it become erect. Then he lowered his head and took the nipple between his lips, toying, teasing, licking, sucking on it. Her body arched toward him. He shifted so that his hand could move further down her body.

Moaning with arousal, she clung to him. He pushed back the satin gown still further, exposing the thatch of hair between her legs. "You drive me to distraction," he muttered hoarsely. "You're a Circe who drives men into danger, aren't you? A temptress who can't be denied."

"Mmmmm."

She was too caught up in the arousal of her body to pay attention to his words. He pulled back from her, teasing. "Do you miss my touch?" he demanded.

"Oh, yes. Don't stop. Please don't stop."

Once again he took her nipple between his lips, sucking the elongated flesh into his mouth. Then he let it slip out. She groaned in protest. His hands were no longer touching her. "I remember how you held me in thrall, years ago. My blood was always at a fever pitch. My need for you was stronger than anything else in the world. You still have that power."

A faint smile curved her lips, her eyes opened languidly. "Yes, I still have that power, Rossmere. But you have the power to satisfy me now. I'm as much under your spell as you are under mine. My body craves to be filled by yours. Don't make me wait," she begged, but with the tone of one who knows her wish will be granted.

He pressed his hand down against the thatch of hair between her legs and lifted it away. "Is this power you have only over me?" he whispered. "I have to know. Are other men bewitched by you? Is your merchant enslaved by his love of you?"

"Oh, yes," she murmured, a knowing smile twisting her lips. "Don't think about him, Stephen. Here, let me help you with your pantaloons."

Rossmere grabbed her hands and pressed them, too tightly for her comfort. "No, no. I can't bear to think of it. He can afford you and I can't. It wouldn't be fair of me."

"But you have the prize money."

He shook his head. "There was some emergency at Longborough. My temporary manager had to have money immediately. So I sent the prize money to him."

"Oh, for God's sake," she snapped. "You don't have to pay bills like some cit, Rossmere." As she spoke, she wrapped the satin gown once more tightly around her. "Really, I lose all patience with you. In the old days you were a great deal more lively."

"In the old days I was a great deal richer," he retorted with bitterness.

Madeline erased the frown from her brow. "Of course you were. It's a great pity, but . . ." She shrugged her slender shoulders and rose from the sofa. "It's very late. I'm sorry we couldn't manage a real reunion, Rossmere. Perhaps your fortunes will change one of these days."

"Most unlikely." He sighed and kissed her firmly on

the lips. "It's not easy to get you off my mind," he said as he picked up the gauntlets he'd left on the table. "Fortunately for me, I'll be returning to Longborough in a while. I trust you'll be happy with your merchant."

"I'll have to be, won't I?"

Rossmere turned abruptly and left the cottage. When the rear door had closed behind him, he drew a deep breath and forced his body to relax before walking into the little woods to reclaim Ascot. It had been a long, long evening.

12

For two nights Jane had sat back and watched Rossmere disappear in the evening. He had made no attempt to explain to her where he was going, nor to report on his activities afterward. On the second evening Jane sat up late in her room, reading a novel and listening for the sounds of Ascot returning to the stables. She drowsed over the book as it got later, forcing her eyes open and stifling huge yawns. It had gone midnight when muffled hoofbeats reached her ears.

Moving to the window, she watched as Rossmere slowed his horse to a walk and circled wide of the house to reach the stables. It upset her that he glanced up toward her window, where not only would he see light still shining but he might well make out her own figure standing there. As if she might be spying on him!

Well, if she was, it was for good reason. She had hoped for help from him, not this questionable absence each night. Where did he go? Certainly not to discover what John Parnham was up to. He could do that better in the daytime. No, it seemed much more likely that he called on Mrs. Fulton. He had the money he had won from the horse race. How much of her time would that buy him? she wondered. Jane was unfamiliar with the cost of such arrangements.

Since he would pass her suite on his way to his room, she snuffed her candle so no trace of light would appear under her door. He might think he was mistaken about seeing her still awake and staring out the window at this late hour. She climbed quickly into bed and lay stiff as a board, listening for sounds of his approach.

It wasn't long before the floorboards creaked with his bold step. One would think the man would at least try to approach silently under the circumstances! But no, he stalked straight down the hall, stopping in front of her bedchamber door to rap twice sharply on it.

Incredible! Did he think she was going to entertain him at this hour of the night? "What is it?" she called after a suitable interval for waking and calming one's nerves, but sounding irritable, of course.

"I need to talk to you," he said without bothering to identify, or excuse, himself.

"I'm in bed."

"Well, you can't have been there long, so throw on a robe and come out here, if you please."

If you please, indeed. His tone certainly gave no indication that he meant to be the least bit polite. Jane did as he asked, though, since she had to know if he had discovered anything about her sister's husband. The robe she slipped into and knotted at her waist was a particularly ancient and unbecoming one of a grayish-green nubby wool. In her sitting room she lit both candles on the mantelpiece before opening the door.

Rossmere was still standing at her bedchamber door and frowned momentarily when she appeared and beckoned him into the next room. "I wouldn't have you in here except that it is even less agreeable to me to discuss matters with you in the hallway," she informed him. "Please have a seat."

As he walked past her to one of the two comfortable

chairs, she caught the smell of a flowerlike scent. Her nose twitched, her lips pursed, she glared at him.

Rossmere turned to find her in this state and cocked his head at her. "I have no intention of molesting you," he assured her. "Is that why you look so disapproving?"

"You've obviously been in close proximity to a particularly fragrant rose bush, Lord Rossmere. Combined with the odor of horseflesh, it's truly remarkable."

He stared haughtily at her for a moment but finally waved a dismissive hand. "Madeline Fulton, of course. I assure you I was there on the most urgent business."

"Urgent," she murmured, unimpressed. Neither of them had yet taken a seat.

"I've spent the last two evenings trying to get information about John Parnham, Lady Jane. Spending the last of my meager resources buying the locals rounds of beer to loosen their tongues."

"I can't imagine how you could possibly have gone through the money you won so quickly."

"It was needed for Longborough." At her look of disbelief, he said, "Oh, never mind that. Just let me tell you what I've learned."

Seating herself, Jane listened with impatience to his tale of the pub and Jem and the horse in the wood. Not even Parnham's horse, she noted. And of his "talk" with Madeline Fulton. Well, it didn't matter to her what he did, did it? The whole story seemed the wildest sort of fabrication, and she told him so.

"You haven't the first reason for believing Mrs. Fulton even knows John Parnham! And don't be alarmed about the depletion of your resources. I shall certainly reimburse you for your expenses on our behalf. All of them," she stressed, her voice strangled with emotion.

For a long moment he did nothing more than study her face. Jane could feel it grow hot under his stare. How unlike her to become so emotional and distempered! If he wished to dally with the Fulton woman, he had every right. Why it should possibly concern her, she didn't know. But it was impossible to meet his cool, unswerving eyes, and she dropped hers to her hands, which lay tightly clenched in her lap.

"Listen carefully to me, Jane," he said with exaggerated patience. "Years ago, when I spent a great deal of time in London, Mrs. Fulton and I had a . . . connection. It was ended long before my financial situation deteriorated, thanks largely to Richard. He had never met her, but he made me talk, made me see what kind of a woman she was. Because she's not just another lightskirt, I promise you."

"I'm quite prepared to believe that."

"She's an enchantress." At her look of amusement, he clenched a fist against the chair arm. "She might have been a great actress. She's remarkably accomplished at playing any role she chooses. But the astonishing thing about her is how clever she is in choosing the role she does play. Without the least hesitation she becomes exactly the kind of woman a man fantasizes about. Demure, or exotic, or untamed—anything at all."

"I presume you know this from your own experience," she said.

"Not just that. When her spell was broken, when she no longer had any hold on my affections, I encountered other men who had known her. Several of them felt they'd had a narrow escape. Most were shipped off by their families to somewhere very far away, or their money was cut off, or some other drastic measure taken to remove them from her vicinity."

"You make her sound like a witch."

"No, not a witch. A very clever, very cunning woman. Though she led a disreputable life, by society's standards, she had every intention of landing herself a husband. She's been incredibly unfortunate up to now, but with Parnham . . . Her patience has worn thin, Jane. She intends to have him, and it doesn't matter that he's already married."

"This is pure speculation." Her hands felt clammy and her head had begun to throb. She didn't want to know that a woman like Madeline Fulton had captivated him, held him in thrall. It made her sick just thinking of it. "You're projecting from your own experience. There's no reason to think that she even knows John Parnham."

He sighed. "Unfortunately, there is. I hate to admit this to you, but years ago I introduced them. The other day, when you mentioned his name, I had a feeling there was some connection I wasn't making. It took me some time to remember the occasion on which I met him. At White's, where we were both playing piquet. Meeting someone at White's is almost a guarantee of their respectability, you know."

"Mmmm. So my brothers say. But I'm sure Mrs. Fulton wasn't in White's."

He frowned at the remark. "No, but it was odd how Parnham showed up the very next time I was out in public with her. Almost as if he'd been waiting for the opportunity. Well, that's mere conjecture. In any case, I did introduce them, and it wasn't long after that that I stopped seeing her. That was the last I heard of either of them."

"Then you have no way of knowing they ever got together."

"Look, Jane," he said reasonably, "it's too much of a coincidence her showing up in this neighborhood, if there isn't some connection. Who else would have brought her here? Not that farmer whose horse was found in the woods, you can bet your life. And who's in a better position to hire a horse from his own tenant farmer than John Parnham?"

"But you're suggesting that he's known her for a long time, that she was his mistress for several years before he married Nancy. That he's brought her out here . . ." Jane stopped, horrified at where this was headed.

"Since the baby was born." Rossmere looked very grim. "Yes. It wasn't safe, but I've told you about Madeline's sorcery. She must have agreed to it because she wanted to be sure of keeping her hold on him. And frankly, Jane, the attempt to convince other people that your sister is losing her reason sounds somehow much more the sort of scheme Madeline would devise than Parnham would."

"Let's assume you're right . . . about everything," she said, feeling a shiver run down her spine. "What are we going to do about it? How are we going to save Nancy? Do you think we could convince my father?"

"We could try, but I'm not at all sure we'd be successful. I tried once before and he was incredibly stubborn, incomprehensible as that is to me. Perhaps you could convince Lady Mabel."

Jane shook her head hopelessly. "She thinks Parnham is a paragon; she won't hear a word against him. Really, it's terribly discouraging. They'll both think I'm being hysterical if I try to make them believe a word of this." She held her head high and tried to swallow the lump in her throat. "I could give Nancy a place to stay. She and William could come to me if I moved into Graywood. John couldn't harm them there."

There was a long moment's silence. One of the candles flickered wildly while the other remained steady. Jane could feel Rossmere's eyes on her, but she kept her gaze locked on his boots.

"It won't do, Jane," he said at length.

"Why not?" She would make it work.

"First, your family and your neighbors would be horrified to see you move into a place of your own. No, don't tell me you would get a companion. You know it's impossible. This is the country, and Graywood isn't five miles from Willow End. There would be incessant gossip."

"Gossip is a great deal easier to bear than the death of one's sister."

"Second," he went on as if she hadn't spoken, "your sister wouldn't come to you there. Parnham wouldn't let her. And he would have the sympathy of the neighbors on his side. He could keep the child from her, too, you know. Don't think that isn't a heavy consideration with her. Why do you think she went home with him?"

Jane's head swung up sharply. "You can't possibly know that."

"I don't know it. I can surmise it. The child belongs to the father, Jane. In this case he would have the court's sympathy, if his wife left him to go live with her sister. You know very well, if you will think about it, that that is exactly what would happen."

Impotent with rage at the injustice of the situation, Jane buried her face in her hands and wept. There was nothing she could do. Nothing, nothing. How could she sit by and watch her sister's husband kill Nancy? Jane wasn't aware at first that Rossmere had moved from his chair, that his strong arms had come around her. He was silent as his hand caressed her neck, rubbing it rhythmically in an attempt to calm her. After a few minutes, the storm of tears abated and she pulled back from his embrace, accepting the handkerchief he offered.

"I beg your pardon," she whispered. "I know that won't do any good."

When she raised her eyes to him, he was already seated in the chair opposite her again. Concern etched two hard lines around his mouth, making him look more formidable than she was accustomed to. In the dim light his blue eyes appeared almost black, and hard, and determined.

His voice was thoughtful. "There *is* one solution I can see."

"What is it?"

"If you and I married and lived at Graywood, we could

probably convince Nancy to live with us and intimidate Parnham into allowing the arrangement, at least for long enough to unearth something derogatory from his past. There must be something wrong there, or he wouldn't have moved into this area."

Jane was staring at him. "Married? Lived at Graywood? You've quite lost me, Lord Rossmere."

"It's been plain Rossmere for days, Jane, and from now on it should be Stephen. I'm sure marrying me is not too great a sacrifice for you to make to save your sister's life."

"But why would you marry me? This is really not a matter that involves you personally."

"Lady Mabel is threatening to cut me off from my only source of funds," he said in the most matter-of-fact manner Jane could imagine.

"That needn't push you into marriage. I've already told you I would be willing to see you have the income from Graywood. It was really quite outrageous of Mabel to try to force you to marry me."

"And I've told you that I won't take charity from you, Jane."

"The property would have been yours! Can't you accept that as reason enough for claiming the income? How does that differ from marrying me and achieving the same result?"

Rossmere raised an admonitory finger. "Let's consider your sister's plight rather than yours or mine, shall we? I think that we, together, could bring it off. Separately . . . Well, there might be a very drastic and unwelcome outcome. Will you at least think about it?"

"I don't know what to say. Surely there must be some other solution." Jane jumped up from her chair and paced to the mantelpiece and back. "It's not that I don't appreciate your offer. Actually, it's much too kind of you. There's no need. Well, no, I don't mean that.

Nancy's safety must be my first consideration, of course, but . . ."

He had risen and stood easily with booted feet spread slightly apart. "Hush. That's enough dithering. You're not a ditherer, Jane. You're a sensible, straightforward young woman. Though you don't like it, you know this is the best we're going to manage for Nancy, and that it's barely enough." He held out a hand to her. "Come here."

An instant wariness gripped her. There was something about the way he stood, something about the look in his eyes. This was not a stringless summons. He intended to add a more sensual element to their relationship. She could tell. It was probably, she assured herself, because he'd just come from that Fulton woman. Yes, that was it. She could read the heightened interest in his eyes, sense the tension in his body, for all its seeming casualness. She would not go to him.

And yet, his desire drew her. She was not unfamiliar with a man's desire. With Richard it had taken only that special light in his eyes to make her own body begin to ache. That couldn't possibly happen with Rossmere. She hardly knew him. It was true that she admired his manly stance and the way he rode Ascot, but that had nothing to do with more intimate matters, nor with the state of her heart, which was irrevocably Richard's.

She found her hand in his and had no idea how it had gotten there. His fingers were warm, reassuring, holding her in a firm grip as he looked into her eyes. Jane couldn't meet his gaze for more than a moment. Her lashes fluttered, her eyes skittered away from him.

"Look at me, Jane."

It took a tremendous effort to do it. And she could feel her hand begin to tremble, her chest tighten, her core swell with anticipation. There was a demand in his eyes, and a promise.

"I'm going to kiss you," he said. "There's no need to

be frightened. It will only be a kiss. I think I must remind you that I'm not merely a dependent of your aunt's, or the owner of Ascot, or the person who can help you rescue your sister. I'm a man offering you marriage, with all that entails. For both of us."

He drew her to him and encircled her with his arms. His mouth descended slowly, coming to rest warmly against hers. She could feel the pull from him, like a tide, drawing on the sensitive parts of her, tugging her toward him. The strength of his attraction was frightening, but she made no attempt to break away from him. It was only a kiss, after all. She was not a fluffy-headed fifteen-year-old to have her head turned by a kiss. By the time he released her, gently setting her a pace back from him, she could barely catch her breath.

"Please consider it, Jane. It's really the only solution."

Before she could think of an answer, he had turned and left the room.

13

Jane spent the better part of the next day trying to avoid Rossmere. It was not that she didn't wish to see him. Indeed, something in her very much longed to see him, if only to ascertain if he would have the same effect on her that he had had the night before. Unlikely, surely. It had been the late hour, the urgency of the situation, the content of his proposal. Marriage! How could she think of marrying him?

How could she not? Her sister's very life might be at stake. Jane knew she would do anything to protect Nancy, but was this drastic measure really necessary? There could be no walking away from a marriage, once made.

And what kind of husband would Rossmere make? He hated the thought of marrying for money, and he would have done it. He obviously found a very different kind of woman appealing. He didn't seem concerned that his own family name and title be carried on to the next generation. In short, he had no reason to marry her at all, except that he needed money.

The only way she could be truly helpful to him financially would be to sell Graywood. Most of the other money she would bring to the marriage would be settled on the next generation, as had been the case with both of her sisters. Not all of it, but a significant portion. And Jane wasn't willing to sell Graywood. It had been Richard's family home and was bound irrevocably in her mind with him, with her sense of his love for her. He had trusted her to maintain the place, to keep it in the family.

And to live with Rossmere there . . . Impossible! She would feel like a traitor to her love. It didn't matter that Richard, who had been an eminently practical man, would have taken one look at the situation and said, "Well, of course you must live there with him." She simply could not do it.

Yet there was a tiny part of her mind, behind all of these considerations, that contemplated it. Not with her permission. And not because it might prove absolutely necessary. Just because of his impact on her. Because she remembered now that her hand had tightened around his waist, that she had wanted to run her fingers through the rough black hair, that the feel of his lips on hers had somehow changed her. She was not, after all, the person who had gone up to her room last night, settled in the knowledge that she would never love anyone other than Richard. A part of her knew better, and whether she agreed to acknowledge that part or not, it was there.

Jane was relatively successful in avoiding the viscount for the day. She could read the amusement in his eyes as she hurriedly passed him in corridors or slipped out of the house to reduce their chances of meeting. She even rode over to Graywood, ostensibly to make sure her tenants were leaving the place in good condition. She made no effort to see the house, but confined herself to an inspection of the grounds after dropping off a cheese for the Browns.

Her tenants had had gardeners to care for the wild woodland glades and great herbaceous borders. The glass houses weren't in use, but the rock garden adjoining the lake had been weeded with care. Jane remembered the rhododendron dell in the spring. She had walked there with Richard, surrounded by the lush pink blossoms. He had stuck one in her hair and laughed at how sticky his fingers got from handling it. He had kissed her in the great walled garden with its pergolas, out of sight of any prying eye.

Oh, Richard. Her throat ached with missing him. The sadness descended on her as usual . . . and yet not quite as usual. There was a distance she hadn't experienced before. As though all of those hours and days spent together were long ago, truly in the past. Stubbornly she protested against the change: it was only a year! She could still remember walking beside him, their arms about each other's waists, laughing, treasuring the good days.

For the first time she realized that Richard's illness had given them more privilege than she had thought. They hadn't had to face the same kind of reality as other people. There had been that one positive aspect. Without the responsibility of marrying and raising a family, they had been able to thumb their noses at society, to abandon the usual conventions, to love each other and share with each other in a way almost unknown to other couples. That freedom could never be duplicated with another man.

It had been a small-enough compensation for all the pain they were forced to endure, her mind insisted. There was no doubt that she'd been spoiled for any other situation, though. Look at Rossmere. The very picture of a cool, self-contained gentleman. What use would he have for a wife, other than as mother of his children, provider of a dowry to get him out of his financial bind? Jane could no more envision him cozily domesticated than she could see Ascot tamed.

Rossmere was not precisely reckless, except perhaps on the horse. But he did have a rather cavalier attitude toward women, if Jane was not mistaken. Oh, sexually he could be tempted by even such an elderly spinster as herself (after a visit to a former mistress), but he would never regard her in the light of beloved companion as Richard had. She and Richard had read books together and discussed ideas; they had had private jokes; they had been able to look honestly at the people and situations around them.

Rossmere wouldn't understand that kind of relationship. In all truth, few men would. Perhaps only a man who was mentally unbalanced, Jane thought bitterly. Oh, if only there were some other way she could protect her sister!

Jane did manage to avoid private conversation with Rossmere for the entire day. She suspected that he was allowing her the time to consider his offer and that he wouldn't be as easy to evade on the following day. When he joined her and Mabel at the breakfast table, a great deal earlier than he usually did, she felt sure he would insist on an interview. Mabel, the soul of determination, rose shortly after he arrived.

"I have a thousand things to do, my dear," she told Jane. "Lord Rossmere, you must certainly try the potted beef and the muffins. A man needs to keep up his strength with a good breakfast, I always say."

When she had hastened from the room, Rossmere regarded Jane with a rueful smile. "She's a very subtle woman, my godmother."

"Isn't she?" Jane sat back in her chair, attempting to look calm. "I'm not in charity with her just now, because she refuses to understand Nancy's danger."

"I daresay that's not the only reason."

True. Another bone of contention was that Aunt Mabel continued to urge Jane to marry Rossmere, but Jane wasn't going to discuss that aspect of the problem. "I have a number of errands to do myself this morning. I'm sure you'll understand if I don't stay with you while you dine."

"No, I really wouldn't understand that," Rossmere

insisted as he helped himself to a muffin from the silver basket on the sideboard. "We really need to talk, you and I. You've had a day to consider my proposal. Even if you haven't come to any firm decision, I'd appreciate your giving me some idea of what your thoughts are on the subject."

Jane met his bold blue eyes uneasily. "My thoughts are quite chaotic, Lord Rossmere."

"If you don't start calling me Stephen, I shall assume the very worst."

"Perhaps that would be best."

His eyes narrowed. "I'm sure it wouldn't. Look, Jane, I don't like to see you squirm. There really is no other solution. The sooner you accept that, the better it will be for all of us, your sister included. I know the idea doesn't sit well with you, and I'm sorry for that."

"It can't sit well with you, either."

He offered a wide, infectious smile. "The idea is growing on me. In fact, it has taken firm root. I've been stubborn and called it natural pride. A man would be frivolous indeed not to consider marriage to you a most felicitous accomplishment."

"Save your pretty phrases for . . . Ascot," she retorted. "We've been discussing a marriage of convenience. I don't want you to pretend that it pleases you any more than it pleases me."

"And I take it that is not at all?"

Jane couldn't tell if this truly disturbed him. The line of his jaw seemed to harden. She deemed it safest not to answer his question. "I've tried to come to some decision. At times I even doubt my own perceptions. What if I've blown the whole situation out of proportion? What if Nancy somehow isn't in danger?"

"Do you really believe that?"

"No."

"Then you must believe that she is. And if she is, the best way to help her is to fall in with my proposal." He watched with a degree of impatience as she shook her head slowly, more in annoyance than in dispute of his words. "You've thought about it, Jane. What other solution is there?"

She could have advanced the old arguments, but it seemed a waste of time. A great rebellion rose in her, however, and she pushed her chair back from the table. "I don't wish to discuss the matter now."

"Ah, well, I can understand that. There are, as you will recall, any number of topics I am unwilling to discuss."

If he was trying to lighten the moment for her, he was totally unsuccessful. Jane frowned at him where he stood holding his filled plate. How could she possibly marry this forceful stranger? It was grossly unfair of fate to deal her another wretched hand of cards.

"I simply cannot answer you now," she declared. "Perhaps tomorrow." And this time she took the opportunity of leaving before he could manage some self-evident and irritating statement of his own.

Jane was informed an hour later by Winters that "Lord Rossmere will not be back until a rather advanced hour."

"But where has he gone?"

Winters cleared his throat. "His lordship did not see fit to advise me of his destination, my lady. Barnes, however, hinted that Ascot would be in grave danger in anyone else's hands in London."

"London! Rossmere has ridden Ascot into London?"

"I believe so, my lady."

Really, it was too bad of him to take off for the city without offering her a word of explanation. Not that she would have stopped him. But if he was going to return that very day, he might have invited her to accompany him. It was always a treat to spend a few hours in London, and Tilly would have provided a perfectly adequate chaperone for the two of them. Jane could have looked at the gowns and hats displayed in the most fashionable shops, or browsed through a museum. She wouldn't have expected Rossmere's company. The trip would have provided a welcome change of pace.

Of course, even if he'd invited her, she could not possibly have gone. For the time being, at least, she must stay at Willow End in case there was any word from Nancy. Or better, she realized suddenly, if she simply removed herself to Parnham Hall. John Parnham could hardly send her packing home, and if she was there, she could be a greater protection for her sister. Why hadn't she thought of this before?

Because it was a temporary, desperate solution, her more rational mind prompted. No more than an attempt to avoid answering Rossmere. Running away, in essence. She could do very little good at Parnham Hall.

Enough to make it worthwhile, she countered as she hurried up the oak staircase. Tilly was in her room, brushing lint from a pelisse Jane had worn the previous day. Jane set her to packing.

"For an extended stay," she said, her tone defiant. Poor Tilly had no idea why, but it didn't matter. Jane had seldom felt such a miserable combination of fear, frustration, and excitement. It would do her good to match her wits against Parnham's. They'd all treated the villain in far too civilized a manner!

When there was a tap at her door, Tilly took the note from Winters and handed it to her. How fortuitous that it should be from Nancy. Jane ripped it open and quickly scanned the sheet. Her heart thudded painfully in her chest. She hastened into the corridor and called after the retreating Winters.

"Is my father in the house?"

"I believe so, Lady Jane. He was in the study not more than half an hour ago."

"Thank you." Jane ran past the startled butler and sped down the stairs, clasping the letter tightly in her hand. The study door was open and she could see her father poring over an old volume spread on his desk. Thrusting her head around the door, she asked, "May I come in?"

"Certainly, my dear, certainly. What's that you're waving about?" He frowned as he recognized the handwriting. "Has Nancy distressed you with something she wrote?"

Jane held a hand up to beg for attention. "Just listen to this, Papa. I know you think Nancy is imagining things, but you have to hear what she's written. And remember that she wrote it to me, not to you." With trembling fingers she straightened out the single sheet of paper and began to read.

" 'My dearest Jane, You've been on my mind a great deal this last day or two. All my life you've done so many things for me that I might hesitate asking yet another, except that you are so good and this is so important. It has to do with William. I have been thinking that if I am unable to care for him . . .' "

Jane's voice caught and she looked up into her father's eyes. "Do you understand that she believes that either she's crazy or that she'll be dead? 'I have been thinking that if I am unable to care for him I would want you to be the one to do it. He's a very good baby and would give you very little trouble, though I realize it would change your life considerably. The nursemaid Sarah would surely be willing to come to you and she's an exceptionally capable girl.' "

The strength of her emotion made Jane pause again. "Well, I won't read you the part about how Parnham is fond of the child but would probably allow me to raise him, at least until he is considerably older. She's probably mistaken on that head, in any case. But her last paragraph is very telling.

" 'Yesterday I walked by the ornamental pond, as I often do of an afternoon. The water was quite clear, with the sun shining off it. As I approached from the garden walk, I could see something in the water, but the glare was in my eyes. I came closer and a kind of terror grew in my heart because I could see more clearly now, and it was certainly a baby there under the water. Of course you will not understand why I immediately thought it was William, but I find that motherhood is like that. Without a thought I leapt over the carved ledge and into the water, which was a great deal deeper than I expected, but only to my waist.' "

Lord Barlow uttered a strangled exclamation but waved Jane to continue.

" 'Before I could even reach the spot where I had seen the baby, there was a great deal of commotion. John was there, and the gardener and his assistant, almost as if everyone had been following my progress. It was John who jumped into the pond after me and handed me out to the gardener. No one would listen to a word I said, but insisted that I was trying to drown myself. Honestly! In such a bit of water, in the middle of the afternoon! But when I looked back, the baby was gone and I let them take me away to the house.' "

Lord Barlow squeezed the bridge of his nose, a pained expression tightening his jaw and drawing down the corners of his mouth. "Ah, poor child, poor child."

"So you think that she is indeed losing her mind, do you? That she has become suicidal?" demanded Jane, irate.

"What is the likelihood that there was a baby in the water?" he returned with a sad sigh. "Try to be reasonable, Jane."

"There's no chance on earth that there was a baby in the water," she admitted. "But I can think of a very different and very likely explanation. John Parnham is trying to convince her that she's crazy, or if not her, at least everyone else around them. What are the chances that her husband *and* the gardener *and* the gardener's assistant would all be there at just the moment she stepped into the pond?"

"He is worried for her safety, Jane. It wouldn't be at all unusual for him to have the staff watching out for her."

"It's just as likely that he had them there as witnesses. That he placed a doll in the water, knowing that Nancy's immediate reaction would be to discover what it was."

"But she admits she thought it was her own child. Preposterous!"

"Under the circumstances, not so odd. Parnham is doing everything he can think of to rattle Nancy. With her nerves on edge, seeing something of that nature would affect her tremendously."

Lord Barlow shook his head. "You're trying to put a decent face on it, Jane, and I think you'd do better to acknowledge the truth. Even Nancy didn't see the baby when she looked back."

"Of course not. Parnham probably kicked the doll out of the way as he 'rescued' her."

"Jane, Jane." Lord Barlow rubbed his temples and sighed. "Perhaps I've done only harm by withholding certain information only Mabel and I know. You and Lord Rossmere seem to think I'm some kind of ogre to believe that Nancy has been mentally unbalanced by her confinement. You might not be so determined to believe her side of the story if you knew of your own mother's problems at the end."

"What do you mean?"

"The last few days of her life your mother was quite out of her mind. She talked of her childhood days as though she were there, and she wept constantly, though not, as far as we could tell, because of how gravely ill she was. She didn't recognize anyone; we didn't let you children see her unless she was asleep."

"Yes, I remember that. But, Papa, she was dying. Something to do with the childbirth itself going wrong."

"Yes, but Nancy's childbirth may have produced similar effect."

143

"But it didn't! I was with her for the first two weeks afterward and there was no sign at all that she was emotionally distraught."

"Except for her crying," her father reminded her. "Remember, you told me how she would burst into tears at the smallest thing."

"But that's perfectly common for women in that condition. You can't equate that with my mother's situation."

"Taken with all the other instances of her strange behavior?" he asked gently. "I'm sorry, Jane, but I have to be realistic."

"My reality is quite different than yours." She stood up to go. "I'm leaving within the hour to visit her. Whether you believe she's becoming insane or I think Parnham is trying to kill her, you must admit that she would benefit from my companionship."

Lord Barlow pursed his lips. "I don't think it's a good idea, Jane. Her husband will take care of her. Certainly I wanted to be the one to attend to your mother."

"It doesn't matter if you agree with me. I'm going to visit her. I'll keep you posted on the situation, from my perspective."

"I wish you wouldn't, Jane. It will only distress you."

She felt weighted down with defeat. "Nonetheless, I can't possibly do otherwise."

"What about Lord Rossmere?"

Her head came up sharply. "He's Aunt Mabel's guest."

But she left a note for him, tucked under his door, before she departed. Wrapped inside it was the note she'd received from her sister. That might serve as some kind of explanation, since she was unable to provide any answer to his proposal.

14

Jane felt a bit of trepidation as the carriage rolled up to the front of Parnham Hall. She'd sent no word ahead of her arrival, convinced that Parnham would put her off if he knew. Determined to stubbornly ignore any hints that she was not welcome, she pulled her bonnet a little closer about her head, retying the yellow ribbon under her chin. If only her coming wouldn't put Nancy in an awkward position . . .

Awkward, indeed! Her husband trying to prove to everyone that she was suicidal was a great deal more awkward than having your sister come to stay uninvited. Jane leaned forward as the carriage drew to a halt before the two-storied porch of the entrance. The hall was an odd building in some ways, with pinnacled turrets and many-mullioned windows. More light came into the inside rooms than in most buildings of Jane's experience, but she had once heard Parnham complain of it. To her mind the light made the large rooms airy and charming, and she loved to picture her sister sitting in one of them with the sun pouring in on her.

Parnham's servants were also an odd assortment. None of them had come with him from the burned-down family home, as far as she could ascertain. At first when Nancy moved to the hall, she had complained of the butler and housekeeper, who were not as accustomed to their positions as those at Willow End. But Parnham had seen no need to replace them, and Nancy had gone along with his judgment. Her high expectations were seldom met, she'd told Jane, but the housekeeper, at least, seemed to make a real effort to improve.

A footman hurried out of the hall and sprang to open the carriage door for Jane. She assumed that the butler had gone to inform Parnham of her arrival, and she walked firmly toward the open door. Over her shoulder she said, "I have two cases. If you would bring them in with you, please."

Before she reached the door, Nancy was there, rushing into her arms, a sparkle of moisture in her eyes. "Oh, Jane, how good of you to come! I never meant to hint that you should, you know," she whispered fiercely against her sister's shoulder. "I just felt that I had to put that in writing."

"I understand. Come, we'll talk in private."

As soon as they were alone, Nancy said, "John's gone off somewhere without leaving any message for me. I can never tell whether he'll be back in a few hours or a few days. It's disconcerting."

An understatement, surely, Jane thought. "Well, we'll do very well in his absence, I daresay. I had visions of him refusing to let me stay here."

Nancy ducked her head between hunched shoulders. "He might have. With a perfectly reasonable excuse, of course: I'm too shaken from my experience yesterday to have company, or some such thing. Oh, Jane, I don't know what to believe."

"Certainly nothing that he tells you," her sister replied briskly. "I don't know how you can bear to stay here with him. Tell me why you returned."

It was as Rossmere had suspected: a threat about the

child. Jane was glad to be able to relieve her sister's mind on that score. "He won't hurt William. That's where his fortune is to come from, being guardian for the boy and holding his money in trust. I'm absolutely positive about that, Nancy."

Nancy's lips quivered but she said nothing. Her jerky movements and distracted expression alarmed her sister. Jane talked to her for a long time, in a soothing, assured voice. She told Nancy about her suspicions and her own suggestions for a solution. When Nancy continued to look numbly disturbed, Jane brought forth Rossmere's much more drastic measures. Nancy stared at her.

"You mustn't consider marrying him just to protect me! How awful for you. Jane, we don't even know if John is this villain you picture. I'm so torn, myself. Except for these wretched occurrences, he's as loving and thoughtful as he ever was. I'm so confused. Perhaps my mind really is distorted."

"Hush! Don't even consider that as a possibility. It's what he wants you to do. Whether you're frightened of him or frightened that you're ill, you're much more likely to act 'irrationally.' I would do anything in my power to protect you, Nancy, including marrying Lord Rossmere."

"I don't see how it could help me for you to marry him."

"Oh, I think he may be right that we could keep you and William safe at Graywood. I have a feeling he would be quite Parnham's match, you know. There's nothing fainthearted about him. I keep thinking there must be some other way," she admitted. "I keep thinking this can't be happening."

"That's how I feel: surely there is some mistake and this is only a nightmare that will come to an end." Nancy clasped her hands in her lap. "Do you like the viscount?"

Jane laughed. "I'm not even sure. Sometimes I do. Sometimes I'm even . . . attracted to him. But I hardly know him and he can be very distant. He was quite adamant about not marrying me for my money when Aunt Mabel first suggested it.''

"Aunt Mabel! She's been matchmaking again?"

"I'm afraid so. She saw it as the perfect arrangement: he needed money and I needed a husband. What could be more reasonable?"

"No doubt she meant it for the best. But, Jane, what about . . . well, your feelings for Richard?"

Jane stared out the window, her eyes unfocused. "I think I'm beginning to accept that with his death those feelings had to change. They aren't as bright and fresh anymore. Now, instead of filling my whole heart, they've condensed into a hard knot as rich as gold but with empty space around them." She brought her gaze back to her sister. "Can you understand that?"

"I think so. Do you think Rossmere could fill that empty space?"

It was a long time before Jane answered. Finally, with a sigh, she said, "Perhaps. Or children could. I can't really know. Just recently I feel that I have to get on with my life and that it's possible that doesn't mean remaining a spinster aunt to my brothers' and sisters' children."

Nancy regarded her clasped hands and spoke in almost a whisper. "I would come to you if you were at Graywood, and married. If it were just you alone, I would fear for both of us, Jane. I'm frightened, so full of fear that sometimes I can't see John at all for the monster that faces me. In my mind, he is no more or less than the devil. I realize that must sound unbalanced, but I can't help but invest him with every element of evil I've ever imagined."

"I don't blame you."

"I feel better now that you've explained that William is probably safe. I don't care so much for myself, but the poor child . . . !"

"You must care for yourself, too, my love," her sister urged. "You see, John's trying to take away that as well.

If you start to believe that you're not worth saving, that there must be something horribly wrong with you if he could do this despicable thing, then you won't fight for your life."

Nancy shuddered, but her hands made a gesture of hopelessness. "Sometimes I can't remember why it matters if he kills me. I get to thinking I must deserve to die."

"How awful! You must stay angry instead of fearful and despondent. Remember that you have a whole family full of people who love you."

"But Papa? He can't even believe what's happening. And you know, Jane—"

"Don't think Papa is against you," Jane said, wrapping a comforting arm around her sister. She explained Lord Barlow's reasons and airily dismissed his doubts. For the rest of the afternoon, she stayed with Nancy, but hard as her sister tried to hide it, Jane could see that her self-confidence was shattered, and there was little she could do to change that.

Since Parnham wasn't back yet, she felt safe enough allowing Nancy to go off alone to dress for dinner, though not to the nursery later. What had happened at Willow End was still firmly planted in her mind. The nursery at Parnham Hall was more conveniently located on the second floor, but in a scarcely used wing of the house. Jane stayed within sight of her sister for the whole evening and begged Nancy to share her room when they went up to bed.

"Parnham isn't here to object," Jane pointed out.

"But what if he returns in the night?"

"If he leaves and returns without warning, he can't very well expect you to be instantly available to him."

"He will, though."

Jane made a disparaging gesture. "I don't think I'd let that bother me overmuch."

"No, but if he's not here, there's nothing to worry about, either."

Against her better judgment, Jane acquiesced to her sister's reasoning. The room she'd been given was a considerable distance from Nancy's, and she disliked the fact that she was not within closer range of her sister's voice. Would she be able to hear a cry for help? Jane fretted about the matter for some time before coming to a decision. She would simply move into a closer room, once the household had settled down.

Nancy and Parnham's suite of rooms consisted of a dressing room for him, next to their bedchamber, and then her sitting room. Both the dressing room and the sitting room were too likely to be used for Jane to enter one of them. Beyond the sitting room was an unused guest room, only rarely pressed into service because of the desire for privacy in the master suite. Jane now tiptoed through the dark corridor in her nightdress, a coverlet wrapped around her, listening carefully for even the slightest sound in the night that might indicate the presence of another person.

In the total silence she opened the door to the guest chamber and it squeaked softly on its hinges. With one last, hasty glance up and down the hall, she slipped into the room and brought the door almost to a closed position behind her. Jane's eyes had grown accustomed to the dark and she could see that the room had only a smattering of furniture: a stripped bed, a utilitarian bureau, and a straight-backed chair. Apparently there had been no call for the extra room during Nancy's tenure at the hall, or it wouldn't have been so desolate.

The bed's headboard was against the wall that adjoined Nancy's sitting room. With any luck Jane would be able to hear voices through the solid partition, even if they reached her only as muted sounds. She arranged herself on the bed with more regard to staying alert than to comfort, despite her exhaustion. If she was going to sleep—and her heavy eyelids indicated that she was—she at least wanted to be ready to spring into action at the slightest indication of trouble. Before she had decided how she would recognize what constituted trouble, she was fast asleep.

Jane found herself in the middle of a nightmare, caught in a web of treachery that caused her heart to pound with fear. The fear made her body jump, shaking her abruptly out of sleep. Dazed, disoriented, she glanced around the room. The emptiness of it seemed almost to fit with her dream, where she had been alone but threatened by something outside the door. Her heart still thumped rapidly and the palms of her hands felt damp. She had to remind herself that it was only a dream.

Gathering the coverlet around her, she slipped off the bed and crossed to the door. Hadn't she left it open? Yes, it still rested against the latch. She pulled it toward her and peered nervously out into the hall. There was nothing there, but by this time Jane felt a strong desire for reassurance. She walked the few steps to Nancy's sitting room and cautiously turned the doorknob. There was no resistance, so she let herself in.

The sitting room was empty. She crossed to the connecting door to the bedchamber. Parnham might have returned, of course, but Jane needed to see for herself that Nancy was safe. If Parnham was there, he was doubtless fast asleep, as there was no sound coming from the room. Once again Jane turned the knob and inched open the door. From where she stood, she could see the big bed, but she couldn't see anyone in it.

Walking carefully, she crept closer, only to discover that her first perception was correct: there was no one in the bed. Jane's heart pounded in her chest. Where could Nancy be?

There was an empty glass on the nightstand. It had the familiar look of the warm milk glass their housekeeper had sent up to comfort them as children on cold nights or when they had difficulty sleeping. Absently Jane picked up the glass and sniffed the dregs. Milk, yes, and beginning to sour. Or was that something else? Odd, the association was just out of reach of her conscious mind. The bitter fragrance sent alarm through her body.

"Nancy?" she called softly, hurrying now out of the room into Parnham's dressing room. It, too, was empty. She hastened past the clothes press and out into the hall, padding down the corridor to the water closet. Empty. Where could her sister have gone? To the nursery? To the kitchen? She would have to check each of them. A sense of urgency was growing in her.

The house was still and her hasty footsteps sounded too loud in her own ears. The nursery was dark and silent, the kitchen deserted. Time was passing, precious time. Being in the kitchen reminded her of the milk at her sister's bedside. They had fresh milk at Parnham Hall, from one of the tenant farmers. Surely it would not have spoiled so quickly, even after being warmed. And that odor, somehow familiar. Jane associated it with the toothache. Hers?

No, Aunt Mabel's. That was it! Her aunt had had a dreadful toothache a year or two previously. Because it was nighttime there was nothing to be done except give her laudanum. Jane remembered distinctly that the Willow End housekeeper had brought some from her own medicine chest and offered it to Lady Mabel in a glass of water. The distinct bitter smell had remained as an elusive memory for Jane.

Would Nancy have put laudanum in her warm milk? Perhaps. She was so distressed by the strange occurrences that she might have sought a temporary oblivion. Or someone else might have offered it to her without her knowledge. Jane's breath caught on the thought. Much more likely that Parnham had something to do with this!

A riot of possibilities suggested themselves to her,

none of them anything but chilling. If Parnham had put laudanum in Nancy's milk and if she was senseless now, then Parnham had to have taken her somewhere. Jane remembered the flight of stairs at Willow End, but knew there was nothing at the hall so steep and dangerous. So where, where, had he taken her?

Jane was standing in the kitchen as these thoughts whirled through her mind. Her absent gaze through the window showed her the kitchen garden in leafy bloom. Nancy was not a featherweight; it would require a strenuous effort to carry her very far. Somewhere in the house, naturally. But Jane's eyes came into focus on the path outside, leading off toward the vegetable gardens. And beyond the vegetable gardens, the shrubbery, with another walk leading to the pond. Oh, God, the pond!

As though in confirmation of her worst fears, she found the door leading to the outside was unlocked. It was not, in fact, completely shut, and Jane pushed it hurriedly open with such violence that it slammed against the bricks of the walls with a loud report. The noise echoed clearly in the quiet night. No sense in trying to disguise her search after that. And besides, it seemed to Jane that the more noise she made now, the better her chances of frightening off Parnham. If she was in time . . .

Never had she run as fast as she ran now. She was unaware of the scrapes on her bare feet as she darted over the bricks. I must be in time, I must be in time, she repeated constantly in her mind as she cried loudly, "Nancy! Nancy! Where are you? I'm coming, Nancy."

Through the vegetable gardens and into the shrubbery, with her breath already coming in shallow gasps. "Nancy!" The shrubbery was never-ending. Its pleasure maze was a torment, with bushes too high to see over, too thick to see through. Not until she rounded the last bend did she have a clear view down the long path that led to the pond.

There was only a sliver of moon casting a pale light on

the scene. As she ran, Jane could hear the disturbed ducks on the pond quacking nervously, and she could see something moving near the edge of the water. "Stop! Nancy! I'm here," she cried in spite of the harsh pounding in her chest. Would she never reach them? She stumbled and recovered herself, ran on.

"It's all right, Jane," said the man who crouched beside her sister's inert body on the ground.

Jane stopped short a few yards away and stared at Rossmere. "What are you doing here? What's happened to Nancy? Where's Parnham?"

The viscount had his hand against Nancy's neck, feeling the pulse beat. "It's slow but steady. I'd guess she's been given some sedative."

"Laudanum. I could smell it in the milk glass, but I couldn't for the longest time remember what it was." Jane dropped down beside him, clasping one of her sister's hands. "Please explain what's going on. I don't understand this."

Rossmere shrugged out of his coat and wrapped it around Nancy's still body. "I think we should get her back to her bed first. Then I promise to tell you what I know." He stood up and reached a hand down to her.

"Yes, of course!" Jane allowed him to grip her hand firmly and to maintain his hold on it once she stood swaying beside him. She was experiencing a reaction to her fear and the exertion of her race through the night: her whole body trembled and her knees barely supported her.

Suddenly she found herself sustained by Rossmere's strong arms around her. In her ear the fierce undercurrent of his voice muttered, "Oh, you foolish, brave woman. Didn't it occur to you that a man so vile would scarcely hesitate to dispose of you, too?"

"No, I'm afraid it didn't," she whispered back. Her hands had gone around his waist, and her head pressed tightly against his shoulder. "It doesn't matter. Nancy is safe. We'll keep her safe, won't we? I won't let her out of my sight until she's safely away from here, Stephen. He mustn't have another chance to hurt her."

She felt the pressure of his lips against her forehead. "We'll keep her safe," he promised.

15

Jane allowed herself to be held for only a minute longer. Poor Nancy lay there in need of their attention. At least she had been too medicated to know what was happening. Even now she slept peacefully on the ground, Rossmere's coat spread over her, her hair tousled and loose on the grass beside the gravel path.

Stepping back from the viscount's comforting arms, Jane said, "She could probably walk if we wakened her." She leaned down to soothe her sister's cheek, but Nancy's eyelids didn't even flicker.

"I can carry her. If you'll just bring my coat . . . and the doll."

Until that moment Jane hadn't noticed the doll lying on the path not far from where Nancy lay. Her startled gaze swung up to Rossmere.

"It was in the pond, as I'm sure you suspected. Kicked under an old hemp sack."

"If you waded in to get it, you must be soaked."

"I've been drier in my life," he admitted as he bent to gather Nancy into his arms. He stood there frowning for a moment. "But don't get up your hopes about being able to point a finger at Parnham for this, Jane. I'm afraid we're no further along than we were before, as far as having any tangible proof of his guilt."

"You didn't see him?" she asked, surprised.

"The man plays his role well." Rossmere cradled Nancy against him and started walking toward the house. "I saw only a masked and caped figure who abandoned Nancy here when he heard the great racket you made."

"I only meant to stop him."

"You did the right thing. It's just that I'm willing to bet we'll find he has half a dozen people ready to swear he could not have left some inn he was putting up at twenty miles from here."

"I see."

The gravel dug ruthlessly into Jane's feet this time as she followed gingerly behind him. It was only just beginning to penetrate her mind that she'd tacitly agreed to marry him. And that whatever tale he had to tell was not going to release her from the necessity. Nancy still had to be protected. The only way they were going to do it, together, was to marry and move into Graywood with her.

His burden didn't seem to bother Rossmere much. Once he paused to shift Nancy slightly in his arms, but otherwise he strode straight for the house. Jane was surprised that no servants had appeared, awakened by her cries. But the kitchen was set way to the rear of the house, with the servants several flights up in the farther wing. There was very little that Parnham had left to chance.

Jane hurried around Rossmere to hold the kitchen door open for him. She locked the door quickly and led the way up to Nancy's chamber. As the viscount laid her sister on the bed, Nancy murmured softly in her stupor. Jane felt a great relief on hearing this evidence that her sister was indeed alive and reasonably well.

"Her color is fine," Rossmere commented as he pulled

the coverlet up to Nancy's shoulders. "I doubt she'll be any worse for her adventure."

"No." Jane brushed the hair back from her sister's face and bit back a desire to weep. Poor Nancy. They could save her from the awful fate Parnham had had in mind for her, but they wouldn't ever be able to restore her life to its previous tranquillity. A ragged sigh escaped her. "Tell me what happened."

After she was seated in a chair close to his, he finally began. "When I returned from London this evening, I found your note and decided the only thing to do was ride straight over here. I didn't bother to tell your father or your aunt, since they would scarcely have understood or approved."

"True," she agreed.

"I'd never been here before, though, and it took me a while to find the place. There was no candlelight shining from any room in the house and no movement outside. I couldn't very well hammer on the door at this hour, so I decided to explore the grounds, keeping an eye out for any indication of trouble."

"How long ago was this?"

"No more than an hour. I wandered around until I found the pond, then waded in to search for the doll. It seemed to me Parnham would have been foolish to remove it right away, in case anyone was around. He'd had last night to accomplish it, though, so I wasn't hopeful. But we were lucky. The doll won't prove anything to anyone else, but it will certainly convince Nancy herself that there's nothing amiss with her mind."

"Thank heaven. She's become quite despondent."

"So I gathered from her note." He glanced over at the resting figure and shook his head. "Poor dear. What a dreadful thing to happen to a trusting young woman." He returned his gaze to Jane's exhausted face. "Let me hasten to the conclusion of my tale so you can get some rest. As I was wading out of the pond, I saw a movement down at the end of the path and quickly hid myself behind the shrubs. It was impossible to tell what was happening because he managed to carry her only a few yards at a time, so encumbered was he by the mask and cape."

"You mean he had the cape wrapped around her?"

"He was wearing it, but it engulfed her, too. An awkward arrangement. It meant I couldn't tell exactly what was going on, but it seemed safe enough to wait for him to get where he was headed. Then suddenly, before they reached the pond, there was the sound of a slamming door and your voice crying out. For a few moments he continued on, but as your voice came closer, he dropped her and bolted off across the gardens before I realized what he was about. I would have followed, except that I couldn't be sure your sister didn't need help."

"Of course. You're not familiar with the place; there are a thousand ways he could have managed to elude you. I'm glad you stayed with Nancy."

Rossmere brushed a finger against her cheek. Her eyes widened slightly but she didn't draw back from the gesture. His voice was cautious as he said, "I went to London to get a special marriage license. We could be married tomorrow if your local clergyman is willing to perform the ceremony."

"Tomorrow?" Suddenly her limbs felt weak again. It was difficult to meet his intent blue eyes. "But I hadn't agreed to marry you."

"It was a precaution. We don't have to use the special license at all, if you'd rather not." His whole hand cupped her chin, holding it so that she faced him directly. "I think we should, Jane."

She moistened her lips and forced a smile, which disappeared instantly. "The tenants at Graywood aren't moving out until the weekend. Would you . . . would we live there with Nancy?"

"For the time being." His hand moved to the back of

her neck, where he rubbed the skin under her thick hair. "I can't take you to Longborough until it's been repaired. I'll have to spend the marriage settlement on that. Unless you'd be willing to sell Graywood."

It was more a question than a statement. Jane mutely shook her head, though which was worse—living at Richard's home or selling it—was a matter of splitting hairs. She was very aware of his fingers and the friction they caused. Her skin became so sensitive that it carried the message of his touch right down through her body, coming to ignite a heat at her core.

"When . . . when we move to Longborough," she said, clearing her throat, "we'll take Nancy with us?"

"Certainly. We've taken responsibility for her, and we'll continue to do so. I wouldn't think of abandoning her, Jane. Ever. She can't come back to this scoundrel, and she'll probably be more comfortable out of this area after a while, anyhow."

As he spoke, his hand moved down her back until she felt him exert pressure to push her out of the chair. With his other hand he guided her onto his lap. And she let him do it, because she knew he would kiss her and she wanted to feel the touch of his lips. Tired as she was, upset, vulnerable, she wanted to cling to him, wanted to press against his strong, solid body. The pulse in her throat fluttered wildly as he wrapped his arms around her.

His lips first touched her forehead and her eyelids, her cheeks and her nose before they reached her mouth. Though they were soft as dew elsewhere, on her own lips they were abruptly demanding. She could feel the heat of him, the persistent pressure drawing a heady response from her. While he nibbled at her lips, his hands moved surely against her back, her hips, holding her tight against him.

The ache grew in her, and with it the need for him to touch her. Her nightdress had slid down one arm, and she made no attempt to adjust it. He traced the bare skin it left exposed.

A shiver passed through her body when his fingers came to rest high on her breast. As his lips reclaimed hers, his hands gradually moved lower, curving down past her breasts. Again a tremor ran through her, pushing her breasts outward as her body arched toward him in a perfectly involuntary movement. His mouth pressed firmly to hers and his hands cupped her breasts, the thumbs posed against the fabric over her sensitive nipples. A breathless need moved her. She made small, unconscious noises as his thumbs pressed, circled, teased.

His tongue was in her mouth, deep against the soft palate. She felt a drawing on her, down, down inside. And one of his hands moved from outside the nightdress to underneath it, his fingers against her skin. The ache increased inside her, grew as his fingers rubbed against her. Her heart hammered in her chest, in her throat, echoing the pulsing need further down. His tongue moved in and out of her mouth, slowly thrusting through her trembling lips; his fingers stroked the tip of her breast until it was firm with her inner need.

And in her shaky state it was enough to bring her to a glittering, pulsing release. She cried out against his shoulder. Her fingers dug into his back, clasping him tightly against her. He rained kisses on her face and neck, rocking her gently as her body calmed into a nerveless frame of skin and bones.

"Tomorrow, I think," he said.

"Yes. Tomorrow will be fine," she agreed.

John Parnham had not put in an appearance before their carriage drew away from the hall. Jane had helped Nancy write a strong note indicating that neither Nancy nor the child William would be returning and that any attempt on Parnham's part to force them would be met with the strongest resistance by Lord Rossmere and Lady

Jane. Nancy held the child firmly and didn't look back at
the house as the vehicle swung from the carriage drive
into the lane beyond. Jane kept a reassuring hand on her
sister's knee.

Rossmere rode behind on Ascot. He would have liked
to stay and face Parnham with his anger, but until he had
married into the family, he hadn't the right. As soon as
he was married to Jane, however, he had every intention
of fully executing his plan to protect Nancy for as long as
she required his services. It was one of the few things he
could do that would help him feel less of a bounder in
marrying Jane for her fortune.

Was he? So many other elements had cropped up to
muddy the water. Not the least of which was the growing
affection he felt for Lady Jane herself. When he'd gotten
her note the previous day and realized she'd gone off to
Parnham Hall alone, the fear he'd felt had been a revelation. It was not only her sister Nancy that he wished to
keep safe. And each time he had held Jane, an absolute
fire blazed in his loins.

She would make a comfortable wife, not one of these
clinging, featherheaded females who expected their husbands to hang about them every hour to provide their
entertainment. Jane had interests of her own and a determination that kept her going when things were difficult.
Her physical desires were certainly all a man could hope
for, and the attendant behavior not in the least missish or
squeamish, both of which attitudes he'd heard were a
great deal prevalent these days. Lady Jane Reedness quite
obviously had a healthy interest in those intimacies that a
husband and wife would share.

Rossmere felt particularly pleased about this. The ma-
jor difficulty of a convenient marriage, in his opinion,
was the necessity for a couple who were not attracted to
each other to indulge in such behavior. It could be nothing but unpleasant for either of them, and positively
loathsome for the woman, he suspected. That Jane was

accepting, even eager, for his caresses was a true advantage to their union. Once it had occurred to him to provide himself with a special license, he had begun to anticipate marriage to Jane with a real interest. If he had used a little physical inducement to encourage her, there was surely no harm in that.

The sun was growing warmer overhead. The rattle of the carriage intruded not at all on his thoughts, and Ascot kept a steady pace without needing a guiding hand. Rossmere was considering what Jane had said to him that morning about her father.

"You know, he might be willing, with the information we can bring him now, to let Nancy stay at Willow End. Even though neither of us actually saw John's face, it is perfectly obvious that it was he. And then there's the doll you found. Together we might convince him to protect Nancy. You wouldn't have to marry me."

"I'm convinced that your father would be a halfhearted protector at best, Jane," he'd said, keeping his voice level with some effort. Didn't she want to marry him? After what they'd been through, it was a bit of a shock to find her backing down. "He'd always wonder if Nancy wasn't truly unbalanced, and he'd find it difficult to withstand Parnham's claims on his own wife."

"I could help strengthen his resolve."

"Have you changed your mind about marrying me?" he asked bluntly. "If you have, you need only say so."

"It's not precisely that. I simply don't wish for you to commit yourself and then find there was no reason. It would be most disagreeable for me to be married to a man who regretted it for the rest of his life."

What an extraordinary woman she was! Rossmere had been somewhat taken aback by her straightforward approach. "I won't regret it," he informed her. "I have a great admiration for you that should form a solid foundation for a satisfactory marriage."

She had studied him for a long moment before nodding. "Thank you. And I've come to trust your judgment, Stephen. Let's continue to be frank with each other, as best we can."

At the time he had thought it a strange qualification, "as best we can." Riding along behind the carriage, he considered her words again and wondered how much they had to do with her former attachment to Richard Bower. Was she saying that she could not possibly be entirely open with him because she would not divulge the extent of that attachment, or how much of it remained to interfere with her loyalty and affection for him?

Irrationally perhaps, Rossmere wanted Jane to love him. He wanted to be the only man she loved. Richard was dead, after all. It was time for her to let go of her fondness for Richard and transfer it to himself. Obviously this was asking more than she was prepared to give. Her attachment to Richard was of many years' standing; she had come to know Rossmere in only the last two weeks. On the other hand, there were her gratitude, her trust, her physical response. All these things encouraged him to believe he would win her heart in time.

He urged Ascot forward until he was riding abreast of the carriage. Through the open window he said, "I'm going to ride ahead and speak with the vicar. If I can induce him to perform the ceremony this evening at Willow End, would that be satisfactory with you?"

Nancy stared at her sister. Jane nodded and said, "Invite him to dinner, Stephen. You know when we dine."

And that was all there was to it. Rossmere tipped his beaver hat at the two ladies and rode off.

16

Jane stood alone in front of her looking glass, gathering the necessary courage to descend to her waiting family. For the occasion she had chosen a white lace dress over a white satin slip, with a corsage of pale rose-colored satin, made tight and cut low. She fingered the row of blond lace that fell over the corsage. Not a very demure dress in which to be married, perhaps, but her favorite, and she was feeling far from demure.

White kid gloves rested on the polished oak surface so familiar to her through all her single years. She had determined not to return to this room tonight. If she couldn't leave Willow End just yet, she could at least have the royal suite prepared for their wedding night, it being unlikely that any royalty would be in need of it for some time.

She drew on the gloves, smoothing them up to her elbows. One would have to be removed when he placed the ring on her finger. The ring. Rossmere had taken her aside just before dinner to confess that he had not had an opportunity to choose one for her, but that if she was willing, she could temporarily wear his signet ring. She dug now in the lacquered box that held her jewelry and took out a ruby ring with a plain gold setting that had been her mother's. Much more appropriate than wearing his signet ring, and somehow less . . . entangling. It was an heirloom and she could continue to wear it, without the necessity of their buying another. The thought of his buying her a ring with her own money once they were married held no appeal for Jane.

Time was passing too quickly now. She had sent her maid Tilly and her Aunt Mabel and Nancy away so she might have a few minutes to herself, but it was time to join the others. With an impatient gesture she straightened the white satin toque and fluffed the escaping curls of shining brown hair. She was annoyed, suddenly, that she wasn't beautiful. There was nothing wrong with her features, of course, except that he would be more likely to adore someone who was beautiful.

Well, this was not a love match, she reminded herself once again. There were many good reasons for their marrying, but being in love was not one of them. Jane clasped the ring tightly in her hand and turned away from the mirror. Odd that she should feel so nervous, under the circumstances. It took a certain amount of effort to move herself toward the door, to open it, to step out into the hall, to walk along to the head of the stairs. Below, the hall blazed with the light of a dozen candles. Winters stood waiting patiently to escort her to the drawing room.

Jane walked slowly down the stairs, lifting her skirts so the white satin shoes wouldn't catch in them. At the bottom Winters smiled at her and said, "If your ladyship will not mind my saying so, you are the image of your mother this evening. She would be very proud of you."

"Thank you, Winters."

Across the hall he opened the door to the drawing room for her and bowed her in. Jane stood a moment on the threshold, regarding each of the occupants in turn. Her father, who had behaved much as Rossmere supposed when they arrived at Willow End with Nancy, was looking rather concerned. He wasn't at all convinced that Rossmere was a worthy-enough husband for her.

Her Aunt Mabel, on the other hand, was beaming with delight. Her careful plans and fondest dreams were being realized. This marriage could not possibly have the disastrous outcome the three young people were insisting had occurred in Nancy's case. If Mabel had been mistaken there—and she was not willing to admit that she had been—this arrangement would more than make up for that misjudgment.

Nancy had skipped dinner, but had insisted on helping Jane dress and appearing for the ceremony. Parnham had shown up in the afternoon with protestations of innocence, hints of her deteriorating mental condition, and "proof" that he could not possibly have been anywhere near the hall last night. Nancy had refused to see him and Lord Barlow had said little. It was Rossmere who had sent him packing, even while Parnham assured him he would be back to claim his wife "when she was a little rested."

Nancy did indeed look exhausted, with dark pouches under her eyes and a pallid face. Jane knew her sister was, at this moment, worried for Jane's sake. Rossmere was largely unknown to Nancy, and he must seem as cool and unapproachable to her as he had to Jane originally. And there was the fear, of course, that Jane was only marrying him to protect her. Yet she stood straight and smiled as Jane entered the room.

It seemed a pity to Jane that her brothers and other sister weren't there for this important occasion. Gathering the whole family together would have taken far too long. She would have to write immediately and invite her siblings and their families home to meet Rossmere, certainly, but not until the bride and groom had a little time to adjust to each other.

The vicar, an old friend of the family, was speaking quietly with Rossmere himself. The two men looked up as Jane moved toward them, gliding elegantly across the room. The Reverend Mr. Winston nodded his white head as though in approval. Rossmere regarded her intently, his face unsmiling. She reached her hand out to him and inconspicuously dropped the ring onto his palm. A flicker of surprise appeared in his eyes, followed by a minute shrug of his shoulders.

"Shall we begin?" Mr. Winston asked.

Jane allowed a moment for any member of the party to object before bringing her gaze to Rossmere's face. "Yes. I think we're all ready."

The vicar was possessed of a most sonorous voice. His manner of declaring the marriage ceremony, which Jane had had occasion to observe more than a dozen times, was impressive and heartening. One would have sworn he had the highest hopes for each couple joined together under his auspices; Jane and Rossmere were no exception. At the conclusion he beamed on them, his mustache bristling with goodwill.

"A long and happy life together," he said. "May you be blessed with many children and grandchildren."

"Thank you." Jane couldn't help but remember that the whole reason she hadn't been able to marry Richard was precisely that. When Rossmere's eyes caught hers, she had the distinct impression he was remembering the same thing. But she refused to look away from him and he took her hand in one of his strong ones.

"We appreciate your agreeing to marry us on such short notice," he said. "Lord Barlow has arranged for champagne to celebrate. I hope you'll join us."

"Nothing would please me more than to drink a toast to the two of you. Lady Jane has long been a mainstay in our parish. I hope you'll be living in the neighborhood."

"At Graywood for a while," Jane said. "But eventually we'll settle at Longborough Park in Sussex. Doesn't your sister live somewhere in that area?"

How simple it was to keep up a social discourse, even

when her mind was on entirely different matters! She acknowledged the toasts and drank rather unsparingly of the champagne. Rossmere hovered close to her the whole time. He was amiable but projected a cool power that forced each of her family members to grant him his new place among them.

Aunt Mabel, of course, was more than ready to welcome him into the bosom of the group. She made a point of addressing Jane coyly as Lady Rossmere, nodding happily at the successful conclusion of her endeavors. Jane hardly knew whether to thank her or scold her for her interference. It proved unnecessary to do either, since Aunt Mabel was far too excited to notice.

Lord Barlow was far more skeptical about the viscount, though Jane realized that he was doing his utmost not to show it. He had said, "You're a sensible girl and you'll make the most of whatever situation you find yourself in, so I shan't worry about you. I just hope this fellow appreciates you."

Did he? Jane really had no idea. Certainly he didn't value her as Richard had. But Richard was gone. She smiled at Nancy and took her sister's cold fingers in her warm ones. "I'm glad you've been here with us for the ceremony, my dear, but it is time you were in bed. You're burned to the socket, poor love."

Nancy nodded and withdrew her hand, offering it to Rossmere. "I wish you both very happy. You shall always have my gratitude, Lord Rossmere. If I can ever be of service to you, you have only to command me."

Rossmere grasped her hand firmly. "I could ask nothing more than that you rest until your strength is recovered. And that you believe I have every intention of taking the best possible care of your sister."

"I'm sure you shall," came Nancy's stout reply as she turned to leave.

In time the vicar left, and Aunt Mabel went along to bed. Shortly afterward Jane found herself headed up the broad staircase alone. She would have to prepare for bed first, with Rossmere following after a further glass of champagne with her father. Tilly waited in the royal suite to help her out of her gown and to brush her hair. As she had been many times before, Jane was grateful that Tilly was not a giddy girl, prone to make teasing remarks on one's wedding night.

There would be gossip in the kitchen about the haste of the marriage, of course, but that didn't bother Jane. Curiosity about the family they served was bound to raise speculation on any number of issues, and if her own wedding helped to keep it from her dear sister for a while, so much the better. Tilly could be trusted to be as discreet as one wished, without infuriating the other servants.

Jane fingered the lacy nightdress she had slipped on with Tilly's help. Earlier in the day Mabel had offered it to her privately, wrapped up in crinkly paper with a ribbon. "I had one made for each of you years ago," she explained, a smug purse to her lips. "Often I've wondered if I would ever have a chance to give you yours."

It was a lovely piece of work, the lace as intricate and beautiful as any Jane had seen. Far too precious to wear to bed, one would have thought. Jane would do so for her aunt's sake, even though there were places where the pattern of the lace allowed a partial view of her body beneath. That seemed rather daring to Jane, since she had known Rossmere for such a short time. Until she remembered the night before and that they had just been declared husband and wife.

They wouldn't have to consummate the union at this juncture, her rational mind insisted. Eventually he would want an heir, but there was plenty of time to get to know each other before that problem arose. Another part of her protested such an ascetic notion as that. Just the thought of Rossmere caused her body to respond with a growing ache. And she suspected that the viscount was more than ready to undertake his husbandly duties.

"Will you be needing anything else, milady?" Tilly asked as she set the hairbrush down with a slight clatter.

"No, thank you. I'll ring for tea in the morning. Or perhaps Lord Rossmere takes hot chocolate. Do you know?"

"No, ma'am. It's Martin who brings him his morning drink."

"Well, I suppose I'll learn all those things in time. Good night, Tilly."

"Good night, Lady Jane, ah, Lady Rossmere. I wish you and his lordship happy."

The girl disappeared quickly from the room, leaving Jane in front of the mirror, her hair streaming thickly down her back over the beautiful white lace. Even in the dim light she could see the reflected swell of her breasts through the lace and wondered what Stephen would think of her displaying herself in such a manner. Would it please or disgust him? She was not, after all, a Madeline Fulton, who probably wore nothing but an emerald necklace for the viscount.

She rose from the stool and walked toward the bed. Where did a bride wait? In the huge four-poster with the covers pulled up to her chin? That seemed so meek, so unadventurous. She could picture herself wearing a lace cap to match the nightdress, tied under her chin with a bow, and looking for all the world like an ailing spinster at her last prayers.

As she stood by the bed debating, she felt a gust of air sweep across the floor and ruffle the hem of her gown. There was no other indication that a door had opened, but her eyes quickly swung to the door leading into the dressing room. Rossmere stood there, fully clothed, watching her. He reached up now to untie his neckcloth with an almost unconscious movement. The starched white linen came away in his hand and slid softly to the floor.

"Would you prefer that I undress in the other room?" he asked, trying to decipher her bemused expression.

"I'm not sure," she admitted. "I feel rather . . . unfamiliar with you."

Jane watched him shrug out of the tight-fitting black swallowtail coat that had set off his shoulders so well. His shoulders looked even more impressive in the white waistcoat and shirt that were revealed. His black satin knee breeches looked suspiciously snug on his muscular thighs. Probably they were her fathers, since it was unlikely Stephen would have brought such full dress for a month's country visit where no formal evening entertainments had been promised.

"You could stop me when I reach a point that makes you feel alarmed," he suggested. His fingers were already busy unbuttoning the white satin waistcoat. When he had removed it, he hung it on a chair back over his coat. "How would that be?"

"That's no way to treat those clothes. Especially if they're my father's," she said, attempting a teasing note in her voice.

"No, they're your brother Samuel's apparently. Martin found them in a trunk in the attic. No one else's were large enough to fit."

"I'm not surprised." Jane held her hand out for the shirt he was just tugging from his arm. In the pale candlelight of the cavernous room she could still see how broad his chest was and its growth of curly black hair. As she carefully folded the shirt, she raised her eyes to his and found him regarding her with acute interest. She'd forgotten how revealing the lace nightdress was. She held his shirt up against her chest.

"You'll crush it," he protested, smiling, as he took it from her unresisting fingers. "Please don't cover yourself. You look charming."

"It's a rather daring garment. Aunt Mabel gave it to me as a wedding gift. I didn't want you to be shocked."

"I don't think you could shock me that way, but I may be mistaken." He placed a hand on each of her upper arms and drew her closer to him. His eyes wandered down over the revealing lace, as his hands gently massaged the bare skin on her arms. After a moment he bent down and kissed her, lingering over the fullness of her lips, nibbling, teasing.

Jane felt an instantaneous response run through her. The edge of alarm that had held her in its grip for several minutes was replaced by an erotic tension that seemed to spring full-blown at his touch. He pulled her body against his, and she could feel the tension in him, the hardness of his desire. And her arms automatically slipped around his waist, so that she clung to him.

For a while they stood that way, savoring the closeness, knowing that in moments they could be fully touching skin to skin. Jane rested her head for a moment against the wiry hairs of his chest, fascinated by their roughness against her smooth cheeks. His hands moved down her back until they came to rest cupping her buttocks. A fresh thrill of arousal sprang up under his fingers. She suppressed a gasp.

"Come," he whispered in her ear. "I think you're not as fastidious as you feared. A little desire goes a long way toward establishing a certain familiarity, does it not?"

"Yes. Shall I wait for you in bed?"

"Please."

Jane scrambled into the four-poster and watched as he removed his knee breeches, his shoes and stockings, and the last undergarment that left him perfectly naked. He had a magnificent male body, broad-shouldered and narrow-waisted, with strong thighs and roughened hands. A thatch of thick black hair rode above his aroused manhood. Jane kept her eyes on him as he approached the bed. Her throat went suddenly dry.

"I think it would be a great pity to crumple your beautiful lace nightdress," he said as he stood looking down at her. "Perhaps if we were to remove it now, it would remain in perfect condition."

Jane moistened her lips and nodded, holding her hands up so that he could lift the lacy confection over her head. He laid it aside with scarcely a glance, returning his gaze to her exposed body. Even the touch of his eyes did something to her, heightening the tension that held her body in its thrall.

"Beautiful," he said simply. He lifted the coverlet and followed the line of her body with his eyes. "How very lovely you are. As elegant undressed as you are fully clothed, my dear Jane." He touched her cheek gently as he climbed in bed beside her. "You're not fearful any longer, are you?"

"No. Perhaps a trifle nervous."

"That's understandable, on your wedding night. Here, lie down beside me." He tossed the coverlet far down on the bed so the two of them lay naked and exposed to the warm night air. Slowly he ran his hands over her body, covering each area of skin with his touch. His hands glided over and then stopped on her breasts, remaining there to rub the rosy nipples into firmness. He rolled them between thumb and forefinger as a sensation blazed down her body to lodge deep within.

His hands followed the trail of the sensation, kneading their way down her satin flesh to the forest of hair and beyond. Before she could even grasp the intensity of her reaction, his mouth had come to rest on one nipple. Again a shock of feeling raced down to meet the new sensations called forth by the hand that spread her legs apart. His lips encircled her nipple, massaging it, suckling it until it was like a cord to her interior, tugging on her very insides, the tension mounting, mounting, with each renewed assault.

He had her legs spread apart and his fingers searched within the soft folds to unveil the entrance to her waiting body. His fingers rubbed a sensitive spot in their search, causing her to moan softly. In order to position himself above her, his mouth left her breast while his hand remained to guide his swollen manhood into the moist opening.

The pleasure Jane had been experiencing was abruptly eclipsed by pain. Her moan of joy turned into a groan of hurt. Rossmere murmured something she didn't hear.

"You're hurting me," she whispered fiercely.

"It will only be a moment. The maidenhead must be broken," he explained, though his voice sounded far away.

Jane was mainly aware of the thrusting, like a goat butting against a wall. Except that he was butting against her, and it was painful. "Ah," she heard him say, an exclamation of satisfaction. She felt no relief. As he stroked through the destroyed maidenhead, each pass felt like scraping a raw wound. Really, this was not at all what she'd had in mind!

With a shudder and a moan of pleasure he collapsed upon her, alternately kissing her lips and whispering endearments. He ran his fingers over her face with a kind of dazed delight. "How wonderful you are," he breathed.

Well, it was their wedding night, and at least one of them was pleased with the way things had gone. Jane reminded herself that she had reason to be grateful that Rossmere had married her. She reminded herself, also, that she had heard tales of painful initiations into marital relations. If she hadn't expected something quite otherwise, she wouldn't be so disappointed right now. Jane managed to caress her husband's shoulder and kiss his cheek with a semblance of happiness.

"You must be exhausted," he said. "It's been a hectic day for you. Sleep well, my dear."

Jane rolled over on her side away from him, but he managed to mold himself along the length of her, his warmth feeling oddly familiar. "Good night," she said. Her voice disappeared into the vast, silent room.

He was already asleep.

17

Rossmere awoke as the light of dawn was growing steadily brighter. He had dreamed of Longborough Park, restored and inviting, with its rooms filled once again with music and laughter. There was a family there, children running through the halls and servants tidying up after them. He would have thought it a dream of his own boyhood except that he had been a solitary child. As one did in dreams, he knew that if he passed through the door of the master suite he would see himself, grown into manhood, as he was in real life. But he would see, also, the woman by whom he had produced all these noisy, happy children. Either the door resisted his efforts, or he was unwilling to make a strong push to gain this knowledge.

Before he could determine which was the case, his eyes blinked open and he found himself contemplating Lady Jane. She slept deeply. The sheet over her came up to her waist. She lay on her stomach so he could see only the smooth whiteness of her back. He was tempted to wake her, or to begin stroking the exposed flesh to arouse her for another erotic encounter, but he remembered that theirs was, after all, a marriage of convenience. Somehow it seemed to him that it would be greedy for him to expect a physical episode again so soon.

Because her vulnerable beauty tempted him, he climbed cautiously out of bed and removed himself to the dressing room, gathering up his clothing along the way. A good gallop on Ascot would alleviate any tensions that were building up in him. It wasn't simply that he would have liked another intimate interlude with his wife; it was that he suddenly *had* a wife. Surely that was the furthest thing from his mind when he came to Willow End. He had deemed himself a perpetual bachelor for many years now, and he had come to enjoy the privilege of solitariness it granted him. Was he going to feel comfortable living with this woman he hardly knew?

The answer scarcely mattered, he decided as he tugged on his riding boots. He was going to be living with her no matter what. The thing to do was to establish his intention of maintaining a certain distance from the conjugal pairing. Not the kind of high-handed disappearing act John Parnham indulged in, of course. That was totally unnecessary. But Rossmere deemed it wise to illustrate from the start that he would keep a great deal of time for himself, for riding, managing his estate, doing whatever he pleased, essentially. Jane must learn from the start that he would not be at her beck and call.

The house was still fairly silent as he descended the back stairs. He unlocked the door out into the summer garden and followed the path toward the stables. Things were more lively there. Barnes started the stable lads hopping at daybreak, since there was more than enough work to keep them busy before breakfast. When Rossmere entered the wooden building, it had already been swept clean of the hay spilled in the process of feeding the horses. He walked directly to Ascot's loose box and rubbed the horse's dark forehead.

Barnes walked spryly to his side, smiling widely. "We hear your lordship and Lady Jane was leg-shackled last night. The lads and I wanted to wish you both happy. There's no better woman on earth than her ladyship, if you'll pardon my saying so. A regular trooper, that one. Has been since she was a bit of a girl."

"Thank you, Barnes. We appreciate your kind thoughts."

"Did you want me to saddle him?" Barnes asked with a nod toward Ascot.

"Yes. I'll take him out for a run."

"You know, there've been those as has asked about that one for a stud since he won the race. I mean, what with the other two being his offspring and all. Just off-hand questions, like, and I didn't want to bother your lordship unless you was interested. He's a wild one to be put to stud."

"Hmm. I hadn't really thought of it. Who's approached you?"

Barnes scratched his head. "Rivers from over Lockley way. And Sir Giles Carson's man just happened to come by this way."

"Sir Giles Carson? He must live more than fifty miles from here." Rossmere was instantly alert. Sir Giles was known for his keen horse sense; he'd been breeding winning racehorses for twenty years. "Does his man often come by here?"

"Never before, to my knowledge. But we all know of him."

"Did he look at Ascot?"

"Asked after him, but your lordship was away with the horse. Seemed real eager to have a look-see. I said I'd tell your lordship and send a message if you was interested."

This last was delivered more in the nature of a question than a statement. Rossmere regarded the black stallion stamping impatiently in his loose box. Why had he never thought of putting Ascot to stud? Probably because he'd never actually raced him before. It was one thing to believe a horse was incredibly fast, another to prove it. There were a lot of people who would pay healthy sums to have a horse of Ascot's attributes service their mares.

"I'll think about it," he said.

But he was already thinking that he had had a way of getting himself out of debt and he hadn't even recognized it. It might not have best pleased him to have Ascot raced regularly, but it hadn't best pleased him to be without a shilling to his name, either. His face remained impassive as he watched Barnes put a bridle on the magnificent beast. When Ascot stood ready, Rossmere swung into the saddle with an excess of energy. He would need a good, hard ride to rid himself of this new sense of dissatisfaction.

Jane was relieved to find herself alone in the huge bed. She thought it was considerate of Rossmere to absent himself this morning when she felt so in need of a warm bath to restore her. So that was what losing one's virginity was all about. Not a very appealing business. There was dried blood on the sheets and on her thighs. Really, whoever invented this ritual might have gotten it a little less messy.

When she rang, Tilly arrived quickly, as though she'd been awaiting the summons. The maid tapped lightly on the door and stuck her head cautiously around it when Jane called to her to come in. "Will you be having your tea now, milady?" she asked.

"Not until I've had a bath. Would you have them send up cans of hot water, please?"

"Right away. And his lordship?" Tilly allowed her eyes to wander toward the door into the dressing room.

"I think he's gone out." Jane could now hear the sound of rapid hoofbeats coming from the direction of the Home Wood. Rossmere's favorite ride, the trail along the wood. She wouldn't have thought of going riding at dawn on the morning after her wedding, but it seemed strangely appropriate for her new spouse. "If he comes in and wants a cup of tea, I'll ring you."

"Very good, ma'am."

Jane was relieved that Rossmere didn't reappear when she was having her bath, but she began to feel a bit uncertain about appearing at the breakfast table to face her Aunt Mabel, Nancy, and her father when her husband hadn't hung around to wish her a good morning. Ah, well, she thought as she allowed Tilly to choose her most youthful walking dress of jonquil muslin, this is not an ordinary marriage and I mustn't expect it to conform to any old-fashioned ideas. And just to add a finishing touch to this sterling piece of rationalization, she added— not aloud of course—that Stephen was not, in truth, the man she would have chosen to marry in the ordinary course of her life.

A man, after all, who knew nothing about antiquities, she reminded herself with a smile. Her humor restored, she proceeded downstairs to breakfast after her usual fashion, ignoring any unspoken questions about where her new mate had gotten himself.

They moved into Graywood two days later. The tenants had treated the house and its contents with remarkable consideration. As Jane walked through the manor, she could see that the Browns had kept the staff at their duties, cleaning and polishing, dusting and rubbing. Though she'd called a few times during the last year, Jane hadn't gone beyond the morning room, with its lovely rosewood sideboard and cabinets.

Now she led Rossmere through the entire house, explaining the history of a portrait or the significance of a ceiling cornice in the form of the Vitruvian scroll. He had visited Richard here and would likely not care about the background she gave, but she felt overwhelmed by the memories that assailed her, and she found it impossible to hide her anxiety in any way other than by imparting this useless information. It never occurred to her that Rossmere would wonder at her intimacy with the house.

As they climbed the staircase, she pointed to a niche, a Georgian addition to the medieval manor house, where a small collection of ornaments in pottery and porcelain rested. "Richard's father was an avid fisherman, and he collected pieces that represented every aspect of fishing. Richard wasn't quite as keen on fishing, but he enjoyed the collection."

"I remember fishing with him once. As I recall, there's a stream that runs through the very southernmost corner of the property."

"Oh, yes, I keep forgetting that you've stayed here." Jane clasped her hands behind her back and continued across the first-floor landing to the southwest room. This was a moderate-size bedroom with a carved beech four-poster bed and several mahogany chests of drawers. When Jane couldn't find anything to say about the room, Rossmere commented, "This is the chamber I occupied. I remember the Dresden mirror. As I recall, Richard's room was the one just down the hall."

"The north room, yes." Jane was terrified that he would suggest they take over the north room. "It's the largest chamber, but not suited to a couple. There's no dressing room or sitting room attached to it. I'm sure we'd be more comfortable in the southeast room."

"Are you?"

"Yes," she said firmly, meeting his bland gaze. "Richard's parents used it, you know."

"I didn't know, actually. Let's have a look at it."

Since this offered the opportunity to skip Richard's room altogether, Jane grabbed at the chance. "The view is out over the lawns and gardens, rather than over the woods," she said as she hurried down the corridor with Rossmere at her heels. Why did she have the feeling he was toying with her? He really hadn't said anything.

Probably it was all her imagination. He couldn't possibly care which room they used. That sort of thing was almost inevitably a wife's choice, in cases such as this, of a temporary nature. Not in an ancestral home, certainly, but Graywood was not his ancestral home. She'd be perfectly willing to share whichever room he chose at Longborough Park.

"I'm rather partial to woods myself, especially with autumn coming soon. The colors will be invigorating, whereas the gardens will be forlorn by then," he suggested as they walked down the corridor side by side.

"Oh, not at all! There's a wonderful burst of color in the autumn. The chrysanthemums and the Michaelmas daisies, the japonica and the Chinese lanterns. It's quite a spectacular display. And before that, just after the main summer flowers are gone, there are the dahlias and sunflowers, the asters and gladioli, the phlox and monkshood, the—"

"As you say," he hastened to interrupt. "I'm sure the view from the southeast room will be everything I could wish for."

"The woods look so desolate after the leaves are gone."

He didn't bother to answer her, but pushed open the door of the bedchamber with a decided negligence. Jane was relieved to see that the room was as delightful as she had remembered. There were beautiful oak floors and paneling, except for one wall, which had a leather wall hanging with a design of swags of fruit and flowers, eagles and monkeys in gold and black on an ivory background. It was a charming item, reputed to have been brought from Spain by Catherine of Aragon. Jane noticed that Rossmere was regarding it with great skepticism.

"Don't you like it?" she asked, surprised. "It must be three hundred years old."

"Not so old as your father's antiquities," he said, his voice light with amusement. "I'm sure I'll come to be very fond of it, especially as it faces the bed."

Jane frowned at the four-poster bed. "That's not where the bed used to be. It would be much more pleasant with a view out the windows, don't you think? Otherwise the hanging could be a bit overpowering."

"An excellent idea." Rossmere nodded at the two doors leading out of the room. "Which is the dressing room and which the sitting room?"

She led him first into the sitting room, with its walnut wardrobe, lady's writing desk, and settee. "This would be my room. I'm particularly fond of the painted Norwegian dower chest, though it's quite modern. From the turn of the century only."

"Terribly modern," he agreed as he followed her back out through the door and across the bedchamber to the other room. "And this would be my private room?"

"Yes." She couldn't tell whether he was pleased, by either his expression or his tone of voice, both of which were totally devoid of clues. She watched his gaze move from the mahogany desk to the bracket clock, from the hanging cabinet to the daybed. "The wardrobe is a Dutch piece."

"How do you know these things?" he demanded, his voice indicating he had reached the end of his patience. "Is it obvious to you from looking at them, or is it family history you're imparting? Richard's family history, that is."

Confused as to what had annoyed him, Jane shrugged off the question. "I've learned a bit about furniture. It's another fascination of mine. Will the suite do?"

"Certainly it will do. Which room will your sister Nancy have?"

Relieved, Jane led him back out into the corridor and past the staircase to the opposite side of the house.

Rossmere had sat down with Lord Barlow and his solicitor, after the wedding, to detail the marriage settlement, and he had gotten better terms than either Margaret's or Nancy's husbands. He knew this because Lord Barlow had attempted to hold him to exactly the same amount of dowry and similar arrangements.

But Jane's was a different circumstance, as was Rossmere's and he had bargained for a much larger amount up front so that he could restore Longborough Park and continue to reclaim it from its debt-ridden position. Jane had insisted on being a party to the final agreement. "It's Graywood that will make the difference," she'd said. "Its rents and its crop earnings will provide a steady income to apply against the Longborough mortgage. I want it agreed from the start that there will be no question of selling it without my full agreement."

There could be no reason other than sentiment that she insisted on holding on to the property. Selling it would have instantly freed Longborough from its oppressive mortgage. Instead, Jane arranged that the estate would be passed on to her children, as if this were the most normal thing in the world. Which only meant that another generation would somehow be bound to Richard Bower and his family. It was almost, Rossmere thought, as if Jane were a widow, rather than a spinster.

The same feeling occurred to him in bed with her. And yet there was no doubt whatsoever that she had been a virgin on their wedding night. Rossmere would have liked to rout Richard's ghost by insisting that they take his bedchamber, but it was more than obvious that Jane found the idea repugnant. If he had insisted, he knew she would have complied, but at a cost to him as well as to herself. He realized that he was not going to banish Richard's ghost by force.

Marriage had conferred on him the privilege of having intimate relations with Jane, but he was reluctant to press this privilege too far. Not that he wasn't eager to indulge the passion that seemed to grow with each encounter. It was Jane's attitude that stopped him, like an invisible barrier. She held her body in readiness for him, but she grew cooler and the less responsive with each experience. The night they moved into Graywood was the worst so far.

Jane wore a light cotton nightdress, nothing like the beautiful and inviting confection she'd worn on their wedding night. She was already in bed when he entered the room in his nightshirt. With careful deliberation she placed a book mark in the volume she was holding and slid it onto a table beside the bed. Her look at him was appraising rather than excited. It lessened his own desire, but didn't extinguish it altogether. She was, to his awakened eyes, a very alluring woman. Her coolness could not penetrate the insistent strength of his need.

"What were you reading?" he asked as he snuffed the candles on the mantel and her table.

"Oh, just a novel my sister loaned to me. Nothing that would interest you."

"You seem to think that nothing you do is of interest to me. My lack of knowledge about antiquities and furniture has misled you."

"Of course it hasn't."

"I am not totally lacking in refinement, my sweet. I'm no stranger to the theater or the opera, and I've been known to read a work of fiction now and again. Recently my life has not offered many opportunities for the first diversions, and the last I somehow lost my taste for after steeping myself in the latest agricultural journals." He climbed into bed but remained on his own side.

"I can quite understand that." She extended her long, thin fingers to touch his shoulder softly. "It can't have been easy to suddenly find yourself without the resources to enjoy London."

He shrugged off her touch. "I hate being patronized, Jane. Wealth is scarcely a criterion for one's value."

She withdrew her fingers. "I think you know I didn't mean that. You've become very prickly about any reference to your financial position. I wish you wouldn't hold it against me that marrying me has changed that."

"It seems to me you're the one who's changed since our marriage. I've always been prickly, as you call it, about having not a sou to my name."

Jane shifted down under the covers. "How have I changed?" she asked.

"You've become cool and distant. Especially in bed."

"I'm right here. You know very well that if you approach me, I will allow you whatever you wish."

"Before we were married, you seemed eager for my approach."

"Before we were married, you approached me in a more acceptable way."

"What the devil is that supposed to mean?" he demanded.

"You were interested in pleasing me then. You aren't any longer."

"Nonsense. You don't know what you're talking about."

Jane stared at him. "I beg your pardon. I know exactly what I'm talking about. Since we've been married, you've done nothing but please yourself. It's hardly a fair exchange for my openness."

"I've done precisely what a man is expected to do. If that doesn't please you, it's surely not my fault."

"There's nothing wrong with me, Stephen, if that's what you're implying. I'm familiar with my body's ability to respond to the proper touch. You have provided very little of the proper touch since our wedding."

"I suppose Richard provided the proper touch," he said bitterly.

Jane refused to discuss that particular matter. "You provided it yourself the night before we were married."

"In lieu of a husband's right to consummate our intimacy. You've been misled about what to expect, because of your particular situation. Since our wedding, I've taught you."

"I don't like being patronized, either, Stephen. I'm trying to explain to you about what would please me. If you're not interested, I won't waste my breath."

"I think you'd best have a talk with your sister," he muttered as he turned his back to her.

"I will."

18

Rossmere had been gone again when she awakened. Well, not exactly. She had awakened when he climbed out of bed, but she had pretended to be sound asleep. There was no sense in talking to him right now. They were both too irritated to reach any compromise. When Jane roused from sleep again, it was later than usual, and she rang for Tilly.

As her maid set down the tea, she asked, "Is my sister up yet, do you know?"

"I saw her going in to breakfast, Lady Ja—Rossmere."

They had all switched to calling her Lady Rossmere, with the usual slips, of course. It sounded so formal, and so final. "Would you ask my sister to come up to me when she's finished?"

As least Nancy hadn't lost her own name by her marriage, since Parnham had not title. Jane sighed, realizing that Nancy had lost a great deal more than that. She was still thinking about her sister's situation when there was a soft tap at the door and Nancy let herself in.

"You look very much the lady of leisure," Nancy assured her as she took a seat at the foot of the bed.

Jane was sitting up against the pillows in her nightdress,

sipping her tea. "I'm pretending it's my honeymoon," she said dryly.

"Pretending? I don't understand."

"Well, Rossmere never seems to be here, so I'm having a honeymoon of my own, you see," Jane explained, not quite truthfully. "How are you settling in? Will you want William's room painted?"

"If you don't mind. It's a bit dingy as it is, not used in so many years. Actually, I'd thought perhaps a cheerful print of wallpaper might be just the thing."

"A lovely idea." Jane set her cup on the table beside the bed. "You be the one to choose the print. But don't on any account leave Graywood without a proper escort. Which probably means Rossmere, for the time being. It wouldn't do for you to run smack into John Parnham in the village and have him pester you. Until we've decided that one of the footmen is to be trusted with your care on such an errand, I'd far prefer you go with Rossmere."

"But it's such an imposition! What will he think of me?"

"He'll think you're a sensible young woman, I promise you."

Nancy sighed and nodded. "I'm sure you're right. How very extraordinary that you were a determined spinster last month and today you're married. If anyone had told me you were going to marry Lord Rossmere then, I'd have thought them quite addle-pated. He's a very handsome man."

"Yes, isn't he?" Jane asked. She bit back the smile that wanted to emerge at this indication of her sister's uncertainty as to anything else positive she could say about Stephen Rossmere. Who was Jane to quibble with her reasoning? Jane wasn't at all certain what to make of him, either. She was staunchly ignoring the signals her heart sent whenever he was anywhere near her. Those excited thuddings were beside the point, if the man couldn't be trusted.

"I have something very, very personal to ask you, Nancy. It's not idle curiosity, but a matter of importance to me. And yet it may embarrass you. The subject is one of which no young lady of refinement would speak."

"Good heavens," her sister exclaimed, a twinkle appearing in her eyes. "It must surely be something of interest, in that case."

"Well, it is something only married women are supposed to know anything about."

Nancy's cheeks blossomed with a pink flush. "Ah, I see."

"If you would rather not discuss it, I will quite understand."

"No, no. I would be willing to tell you what I can, which isn't much, I fear. I never did catch on to what it was all about."

Jane's brows rose at this confession. "You mean, you weren't really an active participant?"

"Yes, that, but also I simply expected something more to happen." Nancy shrugged and made a face. "Since there's little reason to be loyal to someone who has behaved like my husband, I will tell you that each time we were intimate, not much happened at all, for me. John would kiss me and touch me, ahead of time, and then suddenly he would climb on top of me and plunge his, ah, thing into me and I would lie there until it was over. I do understand that is how babies are conceived, so I should be grateful, on behalf of William. But, really, there was something about it that was frightfully disappointing, you know?"

"Yes, I do know. And I don't understand it, either."

"But you're so newly married . . ."

"Oh, that." Jane slid her legs off the bed and into the new slippers waiting there. She lifted her wrap from the chair and tossed it about her shoulders. It was easier not to look at Nancy while she talked, because what she had to say was perhaps just the least bit scandalous. She walked to the window and gazed out over the splendid view she'd promised Rossmere. "I had a great deal of physical contact with Richard. Not a consummation, of course, because of his illness, but we were very attracted to each other and spent a great deal of time together, and . . . things happened."

"My word! I had no idea." Nancy's voice dropped to a whisper that barely reached her sister. "What kind of things?"

"They're a bit embarrassing to describe. But let us say the sort of things that happen before the finale, the kissing, and touching, and hugging and stroking."

"And did you like that?"

"Very much. You see, what would happen was most remarkable." Jane finally turned to face her sister. "After a certain amount of contact, my body would react quite strongly, quite pleasantly. All the tension that had built up would float away on these waves of release. Have you never had that happen?"

Nancy frowned. "It has started to happen a few times, but then the finale, as you call it, sort of stopped it. If you see what I mean."

"Precisely. Did you ever suggest to John that you were disappointed?"

"Oh, no! He was very certain that he was doing what he should. He rather assumed that I either wouldn't care what happened or that I had the same sort of response that he had. And perhaps it's not quite polite for a lady to be so involved. Every once in a while he would refer to my doing my duty. It has a very unpleasant sound to it, that word."

"Doesn't it?" Jane saw Rossmere riding Ascot along the road back to Graywood. She ignored the fact that her pulse speeded up at the sight of him. "Rossmere seems to think that the release should happen from his . . . well, from the finale, just as Parnham did."

"So you think there's something wrong with us?" Nancy asked, surprised.

"I don't know. Perhaps. But does it matter?" Jane regarded her sister with an almost pleading expression. "Why shouldn't we get pleasure from the encounter? I become quite tense awaiting the release, and when it doesn't come, I feel incredibly irritable. You know me, Nancy. As a rule, I'm a very even-tempered person. But since I've been married I've felt very shrewish indeed. Couldn't one's husband make an effort to please one, even if one needed something different than other women?"

"I suppose they can't see why they should. They're getting what they want. Parnham behaved that way about any number of things, and I accepted it because I was his wife. I was raised to obey my husband, not to question him."

"That's not good enough for me," Jane retorted. "If I'd wanted to be frustrated, I could have done it by myself."

"Jane!"

"I'm shocking you." Jane laughed, a mischievous light in her eyes. "It's just that I have gone very much my own way for so many years that I have no intention of crippling myself to adjust to Rossmere. And I see no reason at all why I should. We've made a fair bargain in entering into matrimony; it's no time to start bowing down before all the senseless conventions that would rob either of us of our spirit."

"But his manly pride will be in question."

"Hogwash! What's so remarkable and manly about being able to mate with a defenseless woman? I can see no more merit in it than a woman lying about like a sack of flour while he enters her. If that is what he wants, he shall have it very rarely indeed, for I know a great deal more than some innocent maid who's been brought up on the old wives' tales of doing one's duty."

"You won't make him very happy, Jane."

Jane had a sinking feeling in her stomach. "No, I suppose not, but I can't have less than I had with Richard and still feel right about Stephen as my husband."

It was Nancy who turned aside now. She straightened the ruffled collar of her walking dress with nervous fingers as she asked, "Are you still so attached to Richard that there is no room for a new love in your heart?"

"No. Rossmere has become very important to me." Jane wouldn't admit, even to herself, how important. "But Richard taught me something that I won't ever forget. He said that I must respect myself before I could respect anyone else, and that no one had the right to ask me to give up that self-respect. Not my husband, not my father, not my family. No one."

"But is it asking you to give up your self-respect in just going along with what Rossmere wants?"

"Of course it is." Jane regarded her sister with indignant eyes. "Didn't Parnham try to destroy your self-respect by making you believe he was right and you were wrong?"

"Well, yes, but that's an entirely different matter."

"There are a few similarities," Jane insisted. "Parnham was trying to destroy you; Rossmere is trying to make me deny myself in a different way. I realize he doesn't see it that way, Nancy. That doesn't really matter. I'll keep trying to make him understand. But if he doesn't . . ." She shrugged her shoulders. "Even for him, I won't give up my self-respect."

Nancy's fingers had stilled at her throat. "It seems so little to ask."

"I know. That's why most women would agree to it. And keep agreeing to each of the 'little' things their husbands ask, and their families, and the society in which they live. They will put up with not being educated, with being confined to the house instead of riding about as a man would. So many 'little' things. And in the name of being compliant and good-natured. Well, I, for one, am not interested in being compliant, and I will be good-natured in a way that suits me."

"You have a great deal more courage than I do, Jane."

She smiled then. "I doubt it. At the moment I have more conviction. You'll have enough courage to see you through this troubled time. And I'll be there to help you."

Nancy's jerky movements had smoothed out and her distraction had diminished, but Jane knew she was far from strong. This was no time to show any sign of weakness for her sister to emulate. Having left her husband, Nancy was not going to have an easy life; every level of their country society would frown on her behavior, not knowing what had caused the separation.

"You must indicate by your actions that you had a perfect right to do what you did, whether your neighbors understand or not. You know it, I know it, and a few others will know it. But most of the world won't, and you won't be able to explain to them. You're going to need a great deal of both courage and conviction if you're going to make a reasonably comfortable life for yourself. You'll have to believe that you're worthy of it, that you and William deserve to be happy, no matter what has happened."

"Yes, I can see that." Nancy straightened her shoulders. "Thank heaven I have you as an example. I can hardly bear to think what kind of counsel I would get from Aunt Mabel."

"Never mind. I just tell myself she means well, and then go my own way."

Nancy grasped her sister's hands and squeezed them. "Thank you. I must go now and take William for his outing. Did I tell you we found the most adorable perambulator in the attics? It must have been Richard's."

* * *

Richard, Richard, Richard. Rossmere thought that if he heard the name once more he would throttle whoever dared to utter it. So the man had been a saint! Everyone found it convenient to forget that he was a mad saint. The viscount had no intention whatsoever of becoming a saint and he didn't wish to hear about anyone who had. Richard's shadow, if not his ghost, hung over Graywood like muggy weather.

His servants still worked there, his books were on the shelves, his plans for the crop rotation were still in effect. In the library there was a portrait of him as a lad of ten. Surrounded by dogs, cats, goats, horses, he wore a devil-ish grin and rumpled buckskin breeches. Even then Rich-ard hadn't put up with the standard dressed-up little-boy portraits that were painted in those days.

The hell with him! He was dead. Rossmere was tired of being compared with him by everyone from his wife to the servants. He would be damned it he would let Jane hint at how Richard had pleased her physically. They hadn't even been married! How dare she even allude to such behavior? It he'd known about it, he wouldn't have married her.

In his more reasonable moments he knew that wasn't true. But the reasonable moments dwindled as he stayed on at Graywood. For a few nights Jane allowed him to "take" her, remaining cool and distant. Then a night came when even that changed. She had preceded him upstairs, and he came into their bedchamber smiling his manly reassurance, only to find the bed empty.

Really, it was too much. He stalked to the door of her sitting room and knocked loudly. She called to him to enter. Rossmere found her in her nightdress, sitting up on a daybed that had been squeezed into one corner of the room. "What's the meaning of this?" he demanded. "Why aren't you in our bed?"

"I feel slightly indisposed. Nothing to alarm you, just

enough to not feel up to obliging you with my presence this evening."

That damned reasonable tone of hers was enough to drive a man to distraction. Didn't she have any conception of a wife's proper duties? "I would count it a favor if you would join me," he said shortly.

"It's a favor I can't grant you. Perhaps another night."

Now she really had shocked him. "Surely you don't intend to make a habit of holing up in here," he protested, running a hand roughly through his dark hair. "You're my wife."

"Yes." Her voice was thoughtful. She drew a brush through her hair, regarding him closely as she spoke. "I have no intention of denying you your conjugal privileges. However, every night does seem a bit excessive, when you refuse to honor my wishes in the matter. Someday soon we should discuss the subject and come to some mutually satisfactory decision."

"Someday soon! The devil you say! We will discuss it this minute."

"I think not." Jane rubbed her forehead with those long, thin fingers of hers. "My head is aching abominably, I fear. Perhaps I'm coming down with something."

"You're the healthiest woman I've ever met." He glared at her, but she merely closed her eyes and allowed a pained expression to gather on her face. "Tomorrow. We will discuss the matter tomorrow."

"If I'm well enough," she said feebly.

Two things happened the next morning to prevent Rossmere from pursuing his intention of confronting Jane. A messenger arrived with information about John Parnham that would be useful in keeping Parnham from any threats of removing his wife and son from Graywood. Rossmere had directed his investigation, at Lord Barlow's expense, toward Parnham's previous neighborhood. It had taken more digging than Lord Barlow's original, casual inquiry had set in motion to turn up damaging information about Parnham's reputation and financial dealings.

Without consulting his wife, because he was not in charity with her, Rossmere wrote a note to Nancy's husband that informed him of the outcome of the investigation and strongly suggested that he neither put in an appearance at Graywood, nor trouble his wife further in any way. "Lady Nancy will live with us on a permanent basis," he wrote, "and any interference from you would be most unwelcome and, indeed, most unwise."

Just the proper amount of threat there, he decided as he sealed the single sheet and rang for a messenger to convey it. Jane wouldn't even know, until he deigned to tell her, that he had accomplished this mission. It was, surely, one of the obligations he had undertaken when he married her. She would do well to think again about fulfilling her own obligations in this marriage, he thought with a surge of self-righteousness.

Within the hour a different messenger arrived, with a draft for the agreed-upon marriage-settlement sum. It had not taken Lord Barlow as long as he expected to arrange. Rossmere stared at the check for some time, hardly able to conceive that he would now be able to restore Longborough Park to its former beauty and comfort. It was a project he desired to set in motion at the earliest possible moment, but having been married less than a week . . .

The notion of departing for Longborough Park suddenly took strong possession of his mind. Aside from giving him a chance to start the desired renovations, such a trip would provide the opportunity of teaching his wife a much-needed lesson. If he were to desert her so soon after their nuptials, she would surely regret her incomprehensible behavior and soften her stance toward him.

Rossmere called for his recently acquired valet and directed him to pack for the trip. When the viscount informed his wife, rather stiffly, that he was leaving, she smiled serenely and said, "Have a pleasant journey, Stephen. Don't hurry back on my account. Nancy and I will be very comfortable here together."

19

Jane wasn't nearly as sanguine about Rossmere's leaving as she had let on. With him away, there was no hope of their working out their disagreement. And any separation at this juncture, so early in their marriage, threatened to develop into a permanent estrangement. She would have liked to talk to Nancy about these matters, but she felt Nancy had more than enough problems of her own.

Only with Rossmere's absence did Jane fully realize how attached she had become to him. She missed the deep sound of his voice and the intimacy of his occasional smile. Her fingers itched to lose themselves in his wiry, thick hair and to run boldly over the rough skin of his arms and his chest. Without their battles of wills she felt lethargic, as though only his challenge could fully stimulate her to her best efforts. How perverse of her to miss him because she had no one with whom to argue!

Her Aunt Mabel arrived in the best Willow End carriage two days after Rossmere had departed for his ancestral home. When Mabel was informed of this circumstance, she clasped at her heart. "Surely you haven't driven him off already. I knew I should have spoken with you. It was just that I was sure you knew as much as you needed because of your . . . friendship with Richard. Really, Jane, I cannot believe that you would have the least difficulty adjusting yourself to your marital duties."

"He's gone off to see to the renovation of Longborough Park," her niece protested.

"Nonsense. No man leaves his wife so shortly after their vows have been exchanged unless he is dissatisfied with her physical compliance. You have alienated him, I feel certain of it. Otherwise he would have taken you with him."

Jane shook her head in a rueful gesture that did not reassure her aunt one bit. "Now, where did you come across this important fact about newly wedded gentlemen, I wonder?"

"It won't do the least good to mock my knowledge, young lady. I'll have to think of an excuse to fob off the parish ladies. They'll know just what has happened, you may be sure. I shall say you had to stay here to see to Graywood, since it's been occupied by tenants for the last year. That will help. They'll all know just what tenants can do to a place."

"The poor Browns. How unfair to damage their reputation merely to save mine," Jane teased. "I can't think how you will explain that not a stick of furniture was scratched, not a window broken, and yet they left the place in such abominable condition that I had to deny myself the pleasure of accompanying my husband just to care for the place."

"You've always had such a sharp tongue." Mabel scowled and reached for one of the scones the Graywood cook did so well. Just as she was about to bite into it, her head came up sharply. "It's not because of Richard, is it? You haven't . . . You didn't . . . No purpose would possibly be served by letting Lord Rossmere know of the extent of your contact with Richard."

"Good heavens! What do you know of the extent of my contact with Richard?"

Mabel lifted her shoulders in an exaggeratedly casual movement. "Nothing of significance. I know that you spent a great deal of time with him and that you were far too intelligent to allow things to go, ah, too far." She considered Jane with worried eyes. "It would be most unwise to allude to Richard at all, my dear girl. It's bad enough that you are staying here at Graywood. Of course, Rossmere might very well have inherited it himself. You might point that out. Subtly, of course."

"Sublety is lost on Rossmere, Aunt Mabel."

"Well, when do you expect him back?"

"I haven't the first idea. He didn't mention coming back at all."

A little squeak escaped Mabel. "Don't say such a thing, even in jest. I know what we will do. Yes, yes. The perfect solution. He cannot possibly object and I will arrange everything. What do you say to that?"

Jane laughed. "You haven't told me what it is you're planning, my dear."

Mabel clasped her hands tightly over her chest once again. "We'll invite the family to meet him. In a month's time. Your brothers and sisters couldn't arrange to travel here in any less time than that. Oh, they'll be so delighted to meet your husband. It will make up for their not being at the wedding. And Rossmere would see nothing odd in it. He'll be expecting to meet Samuel and Geoffrey and Margaret. It's the perfect solution."

It was indeed. Even Jane was impressed with the simplicity and effectiveness of her aunt's plan. She impulsively hugged the older woman. "A splendid idea. Only poor Nancy will suffer, I fear. So much explaining to do."

"You worry about yourself and effecting a reconciliation with your husband, Jane. Nancy will manage, I daresay."

Jane forced herself to wait until her aunt had left before sitting down at the writing desk in her room. She penned a letter of exquisite casualness to her husband informing him of the proposed treat. There would be plenty of time for him to get the necessary repairs started at Longborough Park and still return to meet Jane's siblings and their extensive families. No gentleman would be so rude as to avoid a party given in his honor, would he?

A carelessly applied drop of hot sealing wax stung her finger. That will teach me to let myself be distracted, she scolded herself as she sucked the injured finger. For a long moment she stared out the window at the cloudless blue sky, wondering whether Rossmere would give her even a passing thought. Perhaps, after all, he would decide that he needed to have very little to do with her, now that Nancy was safe and he had the means to restore his estate.

But he would want an heir, surely. Having actually gotten married, it seemed only reasonable. Jane was determined that she would not deny him that possibility, despite her feelings on the matter of physical intimacy. How she was going to convey this message, she hadn't the faintest idea. With a sigh she picked up the letter and headed downstairs to find her sister.

Jane spent the next few days restlessly pacing about Graywood, wondering how soon she would have an answer to her letter. She could hardly bring herself to sit with Nancy long enough to work the smallest section of embroidery, or remain patiently waiting while the Graywood housekeeper enumerated the failings of scullery maids or footmen. The house, which had seemed to her for so long associated with Richard, now brought forth only memories of Rossmere. Like a ghost, his remembered image startled her at the head of the stairs or lounging on the sofa. How was it possible for him to have so thoroughly permeated the house when he had spent such a short time there?

Of course it was Jane's mind that was permeated by the desire for his presence, but she refused to acknowledge this until she rode into Lockley one day and found that he was with her every hoofbeat of the way. She had come abreast of Madeline Fulton's house before she realized it, and would have passed by had not its air of desolation somehow impressed itself on her distracted mind.

Every curtain was drawn. The knocker had been removed from the door. No puff of smoke issued from the kitchen chimney. The drooping blooms of the flowers by the gate had not been plucked off for several days. Jane stared at the house for a long moment, uncomprehending. Only gradually was it borne in upon her that Madeline Fulton no longer resided there. A terrible fear seized Jane's heart. What did it mean? Where had she gone?

The first, awful thought that came to mind was that Rossmere, in a fit of irritation with his new, uncooperative wife, had taken her away with him. Ridiculous! And yet Jane somehow felt that it was not such an outrageous thought. Madeline had once been his mistress, and it was easy enough for Jane to believe that anyone who had ever been intimate with Stephen would be more than willing to renew the association, to feel the rush of excitement in his arms. The woman's plans of becoming John Parnham's wife had been pretty well destroyed. Who was to say that she wouldn't have grabbed at the opportunity to join Rossmere?

No, no, no. She was letting her imagination run away with her. Jane pulled her horse and herself up abruptly. Rossmere would never do that. There had to be some other explanation. She switched her gaze to the High Street and motioned to a local boy who stood awaiting the opportunity to hold someone's horse for a penny. He dashed to her in a knock-kneed hurry, grinning with triumph.

"Do you know the lady who lived here?" she asked him.

"Yes, mum. The pretty lady who wore the London bonnets."

An apt description of Mrs. Fulton. Jane nodded. "Do you know where she's gone?"

"Can't say. Wagon came for her things two days past, but she'd a'ready left, see. Took her maid with her, and had Mrs. Holter close up the house."

"Does Mrs. Holter live close by?"

"Just the other side of the village. She goes out reg'lar to some of the big houses but maybe not today. Want I should take you there?"

"Yes, please," Jane agreed, urging her horse to a trot as the boy scampered ahead down the High Street and then off onto a path beyond. Her thoughts swung wildly back and forth between the various possibilities. At the modest cottage where the boy stopped, she dismounted from her mare and handed the reins to her guide.

There was no immediate response to her knock, but after a moment she heard a measured tread approaching the whitewashed door. The woman who appeared before her was someone she'd seen in the village from time to time, a sturdy middle-aged widow who wasn't native to the area. Mrs. Holter dipped a surprised curtsy and wiped her flour-covered hands on her rough cotton apron.

"Begging your parding, my lady," she said. "Didn't know 'twere you."

"Please don't apologize. It is I who have interrupted you. But if you could spare me a moment, there's an important matter I wish to discuss with you."

The woman blinked at her. "With me?"

"About Mrs. Fulton. I had no idea she'd left. The boy told me you'd closed up the house for her."

Mrs. Holter regarded the impishly grinning fellow with

a stern eye. "Wouldn't hurt the lad to be minding his own business, if I say so myself," she grunted as she held the door wider for Lady Jane. "Best come in. It's not grand, but it's clean."

Jane followed her into a bright, spartan room and accepted the chair offered her. "I hope you won't think my curiosity is idle. It's a matter of some importance to me and my family where Mrs. Fulton has gone and if she left with a companion."

"I'm afraid I can't help you much. I was only hired to see that the place was left in good order and that the removers took only Mrs. Fulton's belongings. The cottage was let furnished, you understand, and most of the furniture weren't hers, just certain pieces. She'd already gone when I came in, but her maid had told me when she engaged me that they was leaving the country to settle abroad. Don't rightly know where. Or if Mrs. Fulton went with someone. I do know that she left almost a week ago, on Friday. It was a sudden decision, the maid said. If I knew more, I'd be happy to tell you, my lady."

"Of course. Thank you for your help." Jane rose, trying to appear perfectly calm and satisfied. Friday was the day after Rossmere had left, but it was the greatest nonsense to suppose there was any connection between the two. Something had happened between John Parnham and Madeline Fulton, almost certainly. Perhaps she'd determined that the situation had changed so unfavorably she wasn't willing to wait any longer. Her tale about going abroad was pure fantasy. Why would she do such a thing?

Jane escaped quickly from the house and remounted her horse. As she handed a coin to the boy, the most likely explanation of the circumstances finally won its way through her fears of Rossmere's involvement. Madeline Fulton and John Parnham had run away together. Her sister's husband had probably gathered up his mistress and taken her to live abroad. Poor Nancy! What a scandal to rock the neighborhood and destroy any peace that might have been left to her.

How was she to verify her suspicions? Jane refused to alarm her sister with such news until she was in possession of the facts. She could hardly go to Parnham Hall alone on horseback, though. She'd have to return to Graywood for the carriage and a servant to accompany her. And even then, who was to say she would be able to learn what she wanted? Oh, why had Rossmere gone off and left her to handle these distressing matters by herself?

Urging her mare into a canter on the other side of the village, Jane rode toward Graywood with a heavy heart.

At the stables she was informed that her husband had returned. A burst of pleasure flooded her body, coloring her cheeks and giving a slight tremble to her hands. He had not chosen to stay away from her after all!

Jane hurried into the house, intent on finding him to welcome him home and to impart her surmises. Before she could ask a servant where he was, she caught the sound of his voice in the saloon and pushed open the door.

He was standing near the window with his back to her, wearing buckskins and a riding jacket. His boots were muddy, as though he'd ridden a great distance. It was his voice that halted her on the threshold.

"He's mortgaged the place to the hilt and taken off. With Mrs. Fulton, I fear. It seems likely he's absconded with your dowry, too, though the fellow at the bank wasn't willing to divulge that information. I'm terribly sorry, Nancy." He turned around and caught sight of Jane, beckoning her into the room. "Here's your sister now. I'm sure you'll want her company at a moment like this. If any of my actions precipitated this result, I hope you'll forgive me."

Nancy jumped to her feet and extended her hands to him. Her face was pale but her tone urgent. "Pray don't blame yourself in any way, Rossmere. I'm persuaded that John would have done this, no matter what. You've been very good to me and more concerned than I had any right to expect. Your intention was only to protect me."

Jane watched as Rossmere pressed her sister's hands and dropped them. He met Jane's eyes as he walked toward the door, but she was unable to read his mood. When he had come to Willow End a month ago, she had thought how cool his eyes were, and she thought it now. Where was the warmth for her? She extended a hand to him in an effort to stop his progress. "Stephen, I'm so glad you're back," she murmured.

He regarded her hand blankly for a moment. Then, with a swift, stiff movement he carried it to his lips and kissed it, an oddly formal gesture. "Your sister will explain what has happened. She'll be in need of your comfort." With which he let go of her hand, bowed slightly, and departed.

Only Nancy's need would have kept Jane there at that moment. She wanted to run after him and demand that he speak with her, tell her what had happened, and why he was being so cool toward her. But Nancy stood unhappily in the center of the room, her shoulders slumped, her eyes about to overflow with tears.

Jane moved quickly to clasp her sister in her arms. "Yes, do cry," she insisted. "You've been too brave all along. It will do you the world of good to let out some of that anguish."

The storm of tears that followed would eventually ease Nancy's distress, Jane realized, though it would be some time before Nancy could view this final indignity as anything other than one more tragedy. She clung to Jane for several minutes, then dashed the tears away with her fingers and said, "You don't even know what's happened. I'll try to tell you."

The story unfolded in bits and pieces. From her experiences of the afternoon and the few words she'd caught as she entered the room, Jane could guess the rest, but she let Nancy talk, revealing Rossmere's role in the saga. Jane hadn't known that her husband had sent Parnham a letter before he left, nor that he'd bought a source of information on the household staff at Parnham Hall. Apparently his informant had sent a message alarming enough to bring him back to discover what Nancy's husband was up to.

Jane listened to her sister carefully, absorbing the import of Parnham's treachery: he had taken every shilling onto which he could lay his hands by fair means or foul, and had eloped with Madeline Fulton to the Continent. There would be no more possibility of danger to Nancy, but there would be a lifetime of loneliness and social awkwardness for her.

"And my son," she said sadly, shaking her head. "To grow up under the cloud of such a disgrace. It seems so wretchedly unfair. I don't mind so much for myself, you know, but he will surely suffer."

"Our family will see that no stigma attaches to you," Jane assured her. "Little William will grow up knowing you as his mother, and instead of referring to a father, he will refer to his grandfather. Papa's being an earl will surely help. Things will work out. You'll see. Don't distress yourself on William's account. Probably he'll be spoiled beyond anything by his aunts and uncles and cousins just because he has this social handicap. He'll be everyone's favorite."

"I wish you may be right." Nancy smoothed the crumpled skirt of her gown with restless fingers. "Will you excuse me? It's my time to be with William, and then I should very much like to lie down for a spell." As she rose to leave, she turned to Jane with a smile. "You're very lucky to have a man like Rossmere, my dear. He's tremendously concerned about what has happened, afraid that he may have precipitated John's flight.

Ridiculous, of course, but very dear of him, don't you think?"

"Yes. He's a very conscientious man. Too conscientious, perhaps."

20

Rossmere had managed not to be alone with his wife for most of the day. After dinner, however, when Nancy excused herself to go to her room, he found himself with Jane in the small saloon. He knew she'd tried to seek him out several times, but he had slipped away or ignored the light tap on his door. Now she regarded him with a puzzled expression, her hands folded demurely in her lap, her cheeks rather paler than usual.

"I didn't know you'd found out anything about Parnham's past," she said. "Had you some particular reason for not telling me?"

The days were slightly cooler now. Rossmere closed a window and stood with his back to the dusky light outside. His voice sounded clipped even to his own ears. "Surely there was no need to tell you. I was perfectly capable of handling the matter myself." He flipped a watch out of his pocket to check the time, for all the world as though he had some important engagement. "I had no way of knowing, of course, that your sister's husband would bolt. My threat was merely to keep him from trying to claim either his son or his wife."

"I understand that," she said with her infinite patience. "What I want to learn is why you thought it necessary to exclude me from the process."

His eyes widened. "It never occurred to me to include you." This was not precisely true, but it would serve to demonstrate his point. "I'm not in the habit of consulting anyone before I act."

"I see. You're not in the habit of being married, either, my dear Rossmere. When something so nearly concerns me and my family, I would expect that you would keep me informed of where matters stood."

"Would you?" He raised his brows rather higher than usual to indicate his surprise. "But then, you haven't been married before, either, and have no experience of a husband's prerogatives. I have no need, and no intention, of consulting you on such matters as I can handle myself."

"This is one of the difficulties of marrying in haste. One hadn't the chance to discuss such issues." Jane rose from her chair to pace agitatedly around the room. When she came to a stop, only a few feet from him, her cheeks had regained color, bright spots high on her cheekbones. "It won't do, you know. I'm not a child to be ignored or dismissed. This is all a consequence of my insistence on a satisfactory physical relationship, isn't it?"

"I have no idea what you're talking about."

"Nancy said it would hurt your manly pride. I scoffed at that." She turned away from him and walked to the walnut side table, where she picked up a black porcelain Chinese vase. As she turned it in her hands, she continued to speak. "If the cook had prepared a roast that was not to your liking, you would let it be known what your taste was. Otherwise, how would he know? If I were dissatisfied with the downstairs maid's work, you would expect me to make my objections known. You would consider it quite ridiculous of me to do otherwise. So why is it that you refuse to even hear what I have to say about the process of our joining?"

"You have very little understanding of such matters," he assured her.

"Do you really believe that? And do you think I should settle for being left unrelieved? While you get your own satisfaction?"

"In time you will relax and be comfortable enough with me to experience the kind of release you should feel."

"Will I? I don't think so." Jane set the vase back on the table and turned to face him. "I'm not unfamiliar with my body, Rossmere. I may be unfamiliar with this particular means of sharing intimacy, but I have to tell you that I've experienced the release you speak of with no difficulty on other occasions. This may be a wonderful way of impregnating a woman and it may be a rewarding experience for you, but it is not what I need to achieve relief."

"I don't welcome these hints of your clandestine association with Richard. Had I known of it . . ." He stopped, impressed, before he could finish blurting the hasty words, by the blaze of anger in her eyes.

"Would you not have married me? How very ungenerous of you! Really, you try my patience, Rossmere. Your pride is such a handicap to our being on the best of terms. You think you would like some meek woman who would obey your every dictate, but I assure you you would be bored to tears by her before the day was out. If I hadn't thought you could hold your own with a self-possessed, determined woman, I wouldn't have married you. Because that's what I am. I thought, underneath all that pride and distance, that you had come to admire me a little." Her voice dropped to a whisper. "To even love me a little."

The truth of this stunned him. He could only stare at her. Not until that moment had he realized that he had indeed come to love her, and more than just a little. "Jane . . ." But the proper words wouldn't come at his bidding. He needed to know, first, if she still loved Richard, and he couldn't bring himself to ask her. If he spoke of his feelings, it would put him at a disadvantage in dealing with her demands. She seemed to be waiting for some response, and when he failed, she turned away.

"Then I was mistaken," she said sadly. "It won't be the marriage I had hoped for, after all, but that's not your fault. I read into the situation more than there really was, finding the things I wanted to find. Well, never mind. We'll manage. Most people do. Will you mind that my brothers and sister and their families are coming to meet you?"

He had almost forgotten the letter that arrived along with the information about Parnham. "Of course not." His voice, even his bearing, seemed stiff, and he forced himself to say, "It's kind of your aunt to plan the gathering. No doubt it will mean a great deal of extra effort for her."

"No labor is too great to show off the fruits of her matchmaking," Jane assured him with just the proper note of lightness in her voice. The blaze of anger was gone, the earnest attempt to make him understand her needs abandoned. Rossmere noticed that her hands shook slightly as she straightened a portrait on the wall. "Will you need to go back to Longborough Park again before the reunion?"

"I'm afraid so. I only came to sort out Nancy's affairs. You could come back with me . . ."

"And leave Nancy alone here? That would never do." She walked toward the door, pausing with her hand on the doorknob. "If I were there, I'd insist on helping to make the decisions, you know, so it's better that I remain here. Everything will be quite finished by the time I come, and you won't have to be bothered with my opinions. Good night, Stephen."

There was nothing he could do but let her go. How could he possibly explain that it had never occurred to him to ask her opinion on the restoration of Longborough Park? It was his ancestral home, after all. Just as he had made no effort to interfere in the arrangements at Graywood, he somehow expected her not to concern herself with his home. He had not insisted that she sell Graywood, had he, even though he strongly suspected that her every reason for retaining it was associated with her love for Richard?

A voice within nagged at him that Jane was going to be living at Longborough Park, that she could not possibly wish to be at Graywood now, that she had enough problems to deal with concerning her sister without his adding to her burdens. His pride was indeed keeping them from being happy together, but he couldn't seem to vanquish it.

His pride was all he'd had to see him through the miserable years when his life became a drudgery, without money or friends. Because he'd had to give up all his old acquaintances when he couldn't afford to carouse with them, or even to invite them to rusticate with him in the country. The lack of even a modest income had forced him to cut himself off from everyone of his class, to stand alone, but with his head unbowed. Surely there had been no choice. Now that there was a choice, perhaps, he still found himself chafing, resentful of how he'd acquired the money, aware that everyone would know just how he'd recouped his position.

He'd married money.

When he was caught up in the drama surrounding Nancy, when he was—unknowingly—falling in love with Jane, he had almost forgotten how it would look to the outside world. Even Lady Mabel's threat to cut him off had seemed less important than the other issues surrounding his marriage.

But now. He was able to see his situation with the eyes of the world, and his pride rebelled. He was already indebted to Jane for her money. If he let her have her way in all of these matters, if he let her assume a forceful role in his life, wouldn't it look as though she had bought his compliance?

Suddenly he knew that it made no difference at all. Looking out over the lawn, with darkness falling, he could see the soft outlines of trees and hills. How solid they were, substantial even in the darkness that almost obscured them. When it was so black that they couldn't be distinguished, they would still be there. No matter what the world believed, he would still be the same man.

And Jane the same woman. If he let her be that woman, the one he'd fallen in love with. The one who was self-confident and determined. The one who truly had a spirit of adventure and freedom, unlike the fantasy woman Madeline Fulton could create only as a mirage. Jane had lived her life on her own terms in a much more real sense. Convention hadn't kept her from sharing physical pleasures with Richard, nor would it have forced her into marriage when she didn't wish it.

Rossmere left the small saloon abruptly, allowing the door to slam shut behind him. He took the stairs two at a time, only to find, when he arrived at their bedchamber, that she was not in the bed. There was a note lying folded on the pillow and he snatched it up.

My dear Stephen,
  Please don't think that I intend to deny you the chance to have an heir. However, this would be an inappropriate time, and I'm exhausted. I hope you will give some thought to what I've said and not reach any hasty conclusions about our marriage. Until I see you at Willow End on the 9th, I remain,

Your loving wife,
Jane

Torn between waking her to get to the bottom of the matter and leaving her to a good night's rest, he stood hesitant. Then the sound of whispering voices reached him softly, coming from Jane's sitting room. Her sister was with her, and from the broken rhythm of her speech, Rossmere suspected that she was crying. Jane's low-voiced replies sounded warm and comforting. Nancy obviously needed her help right now, and Rossmere turned to his dressing room with resignation.

Things looked less hopeful to him in the morning. He had spent a restless night, disturbed by fantastic dreams of magnificence crumbling into wretchedness. And Richard had been in one of them, with a woman whose image refused to become clear. Worst of all, he'd reached for Jane in his waking moments, only to realize that she wasn't there. This had happened almost daily at Longborough and he'd hated himself then for his neediness, for the untamed arousal his body achieved at the mere thought of her.

She expected him to leave first thing in the morning and he reluctantly decided to go. Nancy could use all of her attention now; he would wait his turn. And meet her next at Willow End, where Richard's influence would not be so strong.

Before he left he penned a brief note:

My dearest Jane,

We have a great deal to discuss, but your sister needs you now and I left things at a very demanding stage at Longborough. You were quite right as to my sentiments regarding you, and I can only hope that you will find yourself able to reciprocate one day.

Your devoted husband,
Stephen

By the time Jane and Nancy arrived at Willow End, Rossmere's note had pretty well disintegrated. Jane had no idea how many times she'd read it, despite having gotten it by heart within the first hour of receiving it. But she continually went over it, trying to read between the lines, what few of them there were. She had said so many things to him. Couldn't he have been a trifle more specific in the wording about his sentiments? But no, each time there was nothing more there, no clue to his precise meaning.

She could have written to him, insisting that he be more forthcoming. Somehow she chose not to do that. When he told her what he meant, she wanted to be facing him, to read what was in those silver-blue eyes. So she had written him as obscurely as he had written her, and she awaited their meeting. It had seemed forever in coming, and her impatience as the carriage drew up to Willow End was difficult to conceal.

"Oh, look," Nancy cried. "Everyone is here already. How clever of Aunt Mabel to have arranged it that way! Oh, Lord, Jane, have you ever seen Rossmere look so positively handsome? I swear he never wore anything half so distinguished when he was with us before."

Jane stared at her husband, whose eyes were already locked on hers, even as he took her hand to help her down from the carriage. He wore a brass-buttoned blue coat with a buff waistcoat and pantaloons over Hessian boots. His starched white cravat was carefully folded into fashionable falls, and his hair shone like ebony in the afternoon sun. But it was the smile that hovered around his lips that took Jane's breath away. That, and the warm, eager light in his eyes.

"At last," he murmured as he raised her hand to his lips. "And we probably won't get two minutes alone for the next eight hours."

"True," she agreed, terribly aware of the tightness in her chest. "That can't be helped, I'm afraid. Have you met them all? My family?"

"Yes, and they're a gracious collection. No man could ask for a more heartfelt welcome into their circle." He continued to hold her eyes. "They're very concerned about Nancy and have every intention of spiriting her off to visit one family after the other for the next half-year. Will that bother you?"

"Not if I can be where you are, at Graywood or Longborough Park." Her eyes turned earnestly questioning, but there was no time for his answer. She was swept away by her siblings, who laughed and wished her happy and fussed over her. With a helpless glance back at Rossmere, she allowed herself to be borne away to exclaim over how the children had grown and how marvelously clever they had become.

Rossmere was right. The only moments they managed to be alone were the few after dressing for dinner, when Tilly had been excused. Jane held out her hands to her husband. "I've missed you," she said softly.

"And I you. Jane, there's so much I want to say. You look so beautiful. I want to hold you, but Tilly would be furious with me if I crushed your gown, wouldn't she?"

Jane was about to beg him to ignore her gown when there was a hasty tap on the door and a voice called, "If you're ready, Jane, I'll walk downstairs with you. I want to show you the miniature Jasper had made of Liza."

"Later," Rossmere promised, letting go of her hand. "Go with your sister Margaret now."

If she hadn't wanted so much to be with Rossmere, it would have been the perfect evening. Her father was full of goodwill to her and gentleness to Nancy. Her Aunt Mabel was radiant with the success of her scheme. Her siblings played their old word games at the table and included Rossmere with an ease that deeply affected her. Stephen joined in their every pursuit with a lightheartedness she hadn't been positive he possessed. So much laughter and warmth! And his eyes seemed to radiate both, when they came to rest on her, to hold hers with a bold gaze that made her family smile.

Across the room of people his eyes had, eventually, told her that he was willing to wait no longer, and she excused herself, saying that it had been a long day and that she wished to be rested for the next day's planned activities. Rossmere had risen instantly, solicitously, to his feet, made his excuses, and followed her from the room.

"Thank you," he said as the door closed behind them. "I like them all excessively, but I've been away from you too long to be patient for another minute." He drew her into his arms for a long, ardent kiss. "We belong upstairs in our own room, I think."

Rather shakily, she agreed and followed him upstairs to the royal suite. "Don't ring for Tilly," he suggested. "Let me undress you . . . but not until we've talked. You could sit on my lap, though, so I can hold you."

Jane allowed him to pull her down with him into the deep-gold armchair, and to kiss her once, softly, before she drew back to study him. "Would you like me to start?" she asked.

"No, that won't be necessary. I've had a lot of time to think about what you said. And a lot of time to come to understand that pride has nothing to do with the things you've asked of me. I love you, Jane, and I admire you. Not for the world would I hurt you or force you to be less of a person because of my self-consequence. I don't know how I could ever have thought it something desirable to rule over you, like some upstart unsure of his position."

"I think we could do a great deal better than that," she agreed, snuggling against him. "I was pleased when you wrote to consult me on the colors of the rooms. Your floor plan was just a trifle revealing, however."

He cocked his head at her. "How's that?"

"The only piece of furniture you indicated in the whole house was a bed in the master suite."

He laughed and hugged her. "Ah, yes, I can imagine having that on my mind. But, Jane, you haven't told me if you return my regard."

There was a wistful note to his voice that sent a thrill through her. Jane could tell he suspected that she loved him, but he wanted her to confess the extent of her attachment. In some way, without saying so, she had to assure him that he was now the love of her life, that Richard was properly relegated to the past. Not a simple matter, though her feelings were excessively strong and her thoughts were so completely caught up in her husband.

"I love you," she whispered. "I love you so much it takes my breath away. Touching you makes my heart pound, and having you touch me quickens every sense. I have the most wonderful feeling that we belong together, that with you I'll be able to soar above the silly conventions and petty nuisances of our lives." She dipped her head almost shyly. "Does that sound silly?"

"It sounds wonderful to me. I admire your courage and your intelligence and your independence. You'll certainly be able to soar, and I trust that I'll soar with you. But I'm also a great admirer of your body," he admitted as he allowed his hand at last to slide down from her shoulder to the top of her gown, where he traced her flesh with a lingering finger. "I want to make sure that you can soar when we lie together, too. Forgive me for being so single-minded when we discussed it before. Your pleasure really means a great deal to me, Jane.

"You have a wonderfully responsive body," he added, proving it by slipping his finger under the gown to touch her hardening nipple. "It excites me just to know that you delight in your own sensuality. If in the past I've spoken hastily, I hope you'll forgive me."

"There's nothing to forgive. We both found it unsettling to be suddenly married, and unsure of the other's feelings. In future, I hope we'll be more honest with each other." Jane shifted slightly so that his hand was dislodged. His brow went up in a surprised question. "I merely wished to make things a little easier," she said as she started to wriggle out of her gown. "Help me with the fastenings, will you, love?"

"I can't think of anything I'd prefer doing." He regarded her with warm, laughing eyes, their silver-blue color finally coming alive with passionate intensity. "You're the most remarkable woman, my dear. Shall I just remove this last impediment?"

"If you would," Jane murmured.

About the Author

Laura Matthews was born and raised in Pittsburgh, Pennsylvania, but after attending Brown University she moved to San Francisco. Before she sat down to write her first novel, she worked for a spice company, an architecture office and a psychology research project, lived in England for three years, had two children, and sold real estate. Her husband, Paul, has his own architectural practice, and they both work from their home in the Upper Haight Ashbury of San Francisco. Ms. Matthews' favorite pursuits are traveling and scrounging in old bookstores for research material.